Always the One for Me

A Wilder Brothers Novel

Carrie Ann Ryan

ALWAYS THE ONE FOR ME

A WILDER BROTHERS NOVEL

By

Carrie Ann Ryan

Always the One for Me
A Wilder Brothers Love
By: Carrie Ann Ryan
© 2022 Carrie Ann Ryan
eBook 978-1-950443-81-9
Paperback 978-1-950443-82-6

Cover Art by Sweet N Spicy Designs

Praise for Carrie Ann Ryan

"Count on Carrie Ann Ryan for emotional, sexy, character driven stories that capture your heart!" – Carly Phillips, NY Times bestselling author

"Carrie Ann Ryan's romances are my newest addiction! The emotion in her books captures me from the very beginning. The hope and healing hold me close until the end. These love stories will simply sweep you away." ∼ NYT Bestselling Author Deveny Perry

"Carrie Ann Ryan writes the perfect balance of sweet and heat ensuring every story feeds the soul." - Audrey Carlan, #1 New York Times Bestselling Author

"Carrie Ann Ryan never fails to draw readers in with passion, raw sensuality, and characters that pop off the page. Any book by Carrie Ann is an absolute treat." – New York Times Bestselling Author J. Kenner

"Carrie Ann Ryan knows how to pull your heartstrings and make your pulse pound! Her wonderful Redwood Pack series will draw you in and keep you reading long into the night. I can't wait to see what comes next with the new generation, the Talons. Keep them coming, Carrie Ann!" –Lara Adrian, New York Times bestselling author of CRAVE THE NIGHT

"With snarky humor, sizzling love scenes, and brilliant, imaginative worldbuilding, The Dante's Circle series reads as if Carrie Ann Ryan peeked at my personal wish list!" – NYT Bestselling Author, Larissa Ione

"Carrie Ann Ryan writes sexy shifters in a world full of passionate happily-ever-afters." – *New York Times* Bestselling Author Vivian Arend

"Carrie Ann's books are sexy with characters you can't help but love from page one. They are heat and heart blended to perfection." *New York Times* Bestselling Author Jayne Rylon

Carrie Ann Ryan's books are wickedly funny and deliciously hot, with plenty of twists to keep you guessing. They'll keep you up all night!" USA Today Bestselling Author Cari Quinn

"Once again, Carrie Ann Ryan knocks the Dante's Circle series out of the park. The queen of hot, sexy, enthralling paranormal romance, Carrie Ann is an author not to miss!" *New York Times* bestselling Author Marie Harte

ALWAYS THE ONE FOR ME

The Wilder Brothers from NYT Bestselling Author Carrie Ann Ryan continue in this emotionally charged enemies to lovers romance.

It took two days for me to know Kendall was the one for me.

And it took two years for me to realize I had to leave in order to protect her.

When I walked away, I told myself it was for the best. But now we work together, and every time we're in the same room, we end up fighting. If we didn't, we'd end up naked. Or worse–spilling heartbreaking secrets.

If she knew the truth, she'd either walk away for good or convince me to take a second chance. The first thing would break me, and the second would break her. I can't let either of those things happen...

Chapter One

Evan

~Ten Years Earlier

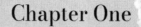

"I can't believe I'm doing this," Keegan announced as he bounced his knee so quickly that it jostled my seat.

I looked over at him while we sat in the airport gate area and studied his face. He might look anxious, but his bright brown eyes were full of excitement and anticipation. He'd shaved his head the day before, the stubble only just now showing up, and still looked a bit danger-ous. That was Keegan for you. "I can't believe you somehow convinced all of us to fly to Vegas for your wedding."

Keegan beamed. "You've always wanted to go to Vegas. And now we're finally old enough that we can go inside the casinos and actually spend money."

I thought about my meager staff sergeant salary, since an E-5 didn't really make as much money as I would've liked. "There's going to be no gambling unless we go to the penny slots."

"Hey, the nickel slots are right there," Ward, our other addition to this party, said from Keegan's side.

I rolled my eyes, my lips lifting at the corners. "Fine, I will go up to nickel slots, but that's it."

"Oh Evan, you're so cute, with your little savings account and truthfully caring about your future," Britney teased as she rolled her eyes and sat on her new husband's lap.

Ward gripped her hip and beamed up at her as if she was his everything. Considering they'd only been married for around two months and, when they weren't working, were constantly boinking each other, maybe they *were* each other's everything.

I was pretty sure they were trying to get pregnant as quickly as possible before we all headed back out for our deployment. But I wasn't going to judge because they looked damn happy.

And with the way that Keegan and Lacey were staring at each other, ready to be married in the next couple of days, I was only slightly jealous.

"A savings account is good," Lacey said as she walked up to Keegan. I moved one seat to the right so she could sit next to him. Britney slid off Ward's lap and took the empty seat next to him as none of us wanted to get kicked out of the airport for inappropriateness.

None of us were flying in uniform, but all of our bags were still those green duffels that couldn't be mistaken for anything else.

The last thing we needed was our chief to hear that we were acting like idiots in public, and then there was no way we'd not get in trouble.

"Yes, a savings account is a good idea," I grumbled.

Lacey cleared her throat. "Well, we *are* saving because we want a future. And we're doing good. I promise we're not going to go crazy and spend too much money."

"That's a good thing," I said with a laugh.

"I'm just sad that Eli couldn't join us," Keegan said after a moment, speaking of my older brother.

I shrugged, missing my brothers, but this was par for the course these days. Keegan and Ward were my brothers now. "He's currently in Korea, so I don't think coming to Vegas for this wedding, however much he wanted to be here, was going to work."

Eli had joined the Air Force before I had and was an officer while I was enlisted. My younger brothers Everett and East had joined up, too, and they were two years into their service.

I had a feeling that Elijah was going to join in the next few months, but we hadn't spoken about it. I wasn't sure if he would try for college or trade school or not, and honestly, I hadn't had time to check in.

I needed to be better about that, but I didn't want to bug him. It was his decision, and our family didn't have the money to send all seven of us to college, which meant that many of us were doing what we thought was right—serving our country and taking the pressure off our parents.

My youngest brother Elliot and my sister Eliza were still in high school, so I didn't know their plans, but it was my job to make sure they never had to deal with too much pressure.

"Okay, so we're getting married, we're going to gamble just a bit, eat way too much buffet food, and be good. No staying out too late and drinking so much that we make poor decisions," Lacey said with a tight nod, as if she were reading off of a checklist. Knowing Lacey, she probably had a checklist and had it memorized. She was the reason we'd all been able to find flights and hotel rooms at a reasonable price to begin with, so I wasn't going to judge.

Britney just rolled her eyes as she giggled into Ward, but I knew that she agreed. We didn't want to get in trouble with a few days off before we had to fly back. Even getting these tickets at the discount rate was strapping us slightly, but this was their wedding, and we were going to make sure that Keegan and Lacey had a great time.

The fact that I was once again flying as a fifth wheel didn't make it any easier.

"Now boarding flight EL855 to Las Vegas International Airport, zone one."

We all began to gather our things, but we didn't stand up or get in the way. We were zone six, and I already had a feeling that the zone sevens were standing at the front of the line, blocking everyone's way.

"I just don't know why they do that," a woman mumbled under her breath near me, and I turned to see a woman with honey-brown hair with blonde highlights and hazel eyes glaring at the line. She had a small bag on her lap and a tiny duffel bag next to her.

"What was that?" I asked, doing my best not to stare. She had high cheekbones, plump lips, and, from what I could tell from how she was sitting, curves that made my mouth water.

I tried not to leer at her because I wasn't an idiot, but it was damn hard not to.

She looked up at me and blinked before blushing. "Did I say that out loud?"

I grinned since I couldn't help it with that sweet face of hers. I cleared my throat, trying not to look like I was staring even though I was. "Yes, but I can ignore it if that would be better."

"No, it's okay." She blushed harder, and I was transfixed. "I am just annoyed that everybody stands up and gathers around the gate all at once as if that would make things go faster."

I snorted, grinning at her. "I was thinking the same thing. They're probably all zone seven."

"And here I am, zone six, just waiting."

I held up my ticket stub. "Zone six here, too."

She smiled at me then. "Good to know. I won't stand up until you do."

"Sounds like a plan. See you then." Ward elbowed me hard in the ribs, and I looked at him. "What?"

"Hot," he mouthed, even as his wife of two months just rolled her eyes and fluttered her eyelashes at him.

I did not want to be the one who got him in trouble,

so I ignored him and turned back to my phone, playing a game while waiting for our zone to be called.

When zone six got called, there were no overhead compartments left, and people were champing at the bit. I just shook my head and walked past Ward and Britney, and then Keegan and Lacey, as they waved to me from their seats.

I was three rows back from them, and I was just glad that we could get two sets of two so that they could sit together. I didn't mind being back here. I had my book and could just relax.

At that thought, I took a look at the person in the window seat and blinked. "Oh. Hi."

The gorgeous woman from before smiled up at me. I'd stood up with her back when they'd called our zone, but we'd all been shuffled around that I'd lost sight of her until now. "Hi. Are you the middle seat or the row seat?"

I looked at my ticket and then up at the bulkhead. "The middle seat. Great," I grumbled and took my place.

She winced. "Both of my bags fit under the seat in front of me, but if I'm taking up too much space, just let me know."

I shook my head and stuffed my small bag underneath the seat next to hers. "It's fine. We're good."

An older man with headphones in his ears and his phone in his hands took the seat next to me without a word, crossed his feet in front of him, folded his arms on his chest, and promptly fell asleep.

I looked over at him, shook my head, and then smiled at the woman who I seemingly couldn't get enough of. "I wish I could do that."

She looked past me, her teeth biting into that very bitable lip. "I can't sleep on trips either. I try, though."

"Well, I won't bother you then," I said quickly, worried that she was trying to be pointed with her remark. I moved a bit, trying to get comfortable. I was a big man, over six feet, and broad with muscles, but the girl next to me and the older man were both small enough that they weren't taking up any space.

Instead, I was the bull in the China shop.

"I'm not going to sleep anyway. I'm just going to try to read. You too?" she asked, looking down at my phone.

I pulled up my e-reader and waved it. "I'll try."

"I'm Kendall, by the way," she whispered, and I looked down at her, my heart racing. Why was it doing that? I'd seen and been with my share of beautiful woman...but there was just something about her.

"Evan."

"It's nice to meet you, Evan."

"Likewise."

8

I wouldn't know until later that this flight changed my destiny.

* * *

I couldn't stop talking to Kendall. Though I was trying to be quiet, I knew that others around us could probably hear my rough chuckle and her sweet laugh.

Her eyes brightened as we shared a ginger ale, since we were near the back of the plane and they had already run out of most sodas when they got to us. I just shook my head and opened my bag of peanuts so she could have them.

"So, what are you heading to Vegas for?" I asked as we did our best to relax.

"I'm meeting my family for a vacation." She rolled her eyes, and I frowned.

"Vegas isn't something that you wanted to do?"

"Considering my older brother can go into places, and my parents love gambling, I can't really do much since I'm only twenty."

That made me blink since that might be legal, but I was still a couple of years older than her. Plus going to Vegas under twenty-one didn't make much sense. "Oh."

"Yes, I'm an adult, but not adult enough to have a drink or walk into a casino, which is fine. I'll just go drive to the Hoover Dam or something with our rental car, but it's not the same."

"I don't know if Vegas is worth it for anyone under twenty-one."

"That's what I said, but I didn't get a vote." She shrugged. "It's not that big of a deal. They have already been out there a couple of days. I came in later because I had to finish up my exams."

"College then?" I asked.

"Yes, I'm trying to at least do a business degree before I think about if I want to go into culinary school or not." She pressed her lips together. "Once again, I didn't mean to actually say that out loud."

"Culinary school?" I could barely boil water.

"I love it. I love cooking. It's what I want to do, but my parents made me try for business first so I could follow in my dad's footsteps. He's an 'entrepreneur,' as he likes to say," she said with a roll of her eyes.

There was a story there, but sitting in a metal tin can in the air surrounded by other people wasn't the best place to ask about it. "I followed in my family's footsteps too, but the Air Force isn't exactly the same."

She smiled up at me, and my heart flipped. What the hell? *Flipped?* "I noticed the hair and the bag, and I assumed, but I didn't know what branch."

I shrugged, which was hard to do in a middle seat.

"Nobody ever actually thinks of Air Force. It's usually Army or Marine."

"Considering how many bases there in San Antonio, you could be anything."

My gaze kept traveling to her hands and the way she gripped them in front of her. They looked soft, and it was all I could do not to reach out and touch her. What the hell was wrong with me? "That's true, but I'm at Lackland."

She frowned, then nodded. "I know that base. Although I'm closer to Randolph."

My lips twitched. "Look at you, knowing the names of bases."

"It's kind of hard not to when you live near them."

She smiled then, and we talked a bit more, and when the plane hit a bit of turbulence, her eyes widened, and she gripped my hand. I looked down at her soft skin touching mine and swallowed hard.

"Shit. You okay?" I cringed. "I should probably not curse."

"Cursing is fine, but maybe not in public where people can get all grouchy. And if it keeps me from worrying about this plane turning into a fiery ball of nothingness as we die screaming, I'm fine with that."

I just stared at her before I laughed, the plane shaking a bit more. "Well, that's an image."

"I blame the movie *Final Destination*."

I shuddered. "I still can't drive behind anything with those white poles, the piping, or logs."

"Exactly. No, thank you." She smiled, even as the planed moved, and she squeezed my hand harder.

I stared at her then and wondered why I had to find her here. Now. On an airplane when we were going to Las Vegas of all places.

"Where are you guys staying?" she asked after a minute, the plane continuing to shake.

"The Rio. Not the greatest hotel, not even directly on the Strip, but we had to take what we could get."

"We're at the Venetian, which sounds fancier than it is."

Not in my opinion, but I didn't say that. "Maybe I'll see you around," I said after a minute, wanting to bite my own tongue off.

"Maybe. I'll be the one walking around the casino rather than through it," she whined.

I raised a brow. "Do you really want to gamble?"

"Not really. I do want to see a show or something. I haven't really thought about it. I've been so worried about exams that I didn't get to plan this vacation."

That brought up an idea that sounded insane. "If your parents don't mind, and you find yourself bored, you should come and hang out with us."

"Are you serious?" she whispered, her eyes wide.

I hadn't even meant to say the words, but then they were out, and there was no going back.

* * *

And that was how I found myself laughing hysterically as I walked down the Strip, Kendall by my side, as Britney and Lacey regaled her with stories about me.

I should've stopped them, should've tried not to be the center of attention, but I didn't care right then.

It was just nice to laugh, to not feel like the fifth wheel.

"Seriously though, he was just in his boxer briefs, snow was coming down, and he was standing there, pretending to shovel." Lacey rolled her eyes.

"That snowstorm did startle all of us," Kendall said after a minute. "It doesn't snow in San Antonio."

"No, and people don't know how to drive in it or handle it, but Evan had to go out in his boxers to take care of it."

"It was on a dare, it was less than thirty seconds, and I quickly came in and got dressed so I didn't die of hypothermia. I'm not an idiot."

Kendall raised a brow. "I didn't think you were, and I would've hoped it was a dare. Or you were drunk."

"You can blame us for that," Ward said, grinning.

"Seriously though, he did win the bet." Keegan grinned.

I just shook my head as we walked around the Strip, each of us eating way too much food wherever we stopped.

"We're going to go do a penny slot, just to say we did."

I looked down at Kendall, who blushed, embarrassed. "I'm going to stand out here with Kendall, so she doesn't end up in jail." She elbowed me in the gut, and I let out a breath. "Ow, pointy elbow."

"Don't make fun of my elbows or my age. I'm twenty, not seventeen."

Thank God for that. I at least thought that to myself and didn't say it out loud.

That night we went to a show, something with magic that was off the Strip, cheap, and made us laugh. They weren't carding anybody, so Kendall was able to have a drink. Although we tried not to be suspicious about it, I knew that she wasn't the only underage person in here. We were laughing too hard, getting a little too drunk, but having way too much fun.

Later that night, I walked her to the Venetian, and as the lights twinkled, music blared, and people milled about us, I cupped her face and pressed my lips to hers.

We were drunk, but not too drunk, and when I moaned against her, she wrapped her arms around my waist and then smiled up at me.

"I'm delighted that I met you, Evan."

"Damn straight," I whispered, my breath going choppy. I pressed my forehead to hers and smiled. "Tomorrow then?"

"Tomorrow is bachelor and bachelorette time. The girls invited me." She beamed, her entire face lighting up, and I swore I fell in love.

"They like you."

I like you too.

"I like them too. So yes, my parents are excited that I'm not hanging out with them because that means they can do what they want, and my brother too."

I didn't know her family and hadn't met them, but I already didn't like them. "While that kind of annoys me, I'm going to pretend that it doesn't because I get to spend time with you."

"Evan," she whispered, and I realized I had said that out loud.

I kissed her again, tucked her hair behind her ear, and then watched as she safely made her way into the hotel and to the elevators.

I stuck my hands in my pockets and watched after she was out of sight for longer than I should have. I was grateful when she texted to tell me she was safe in her room.

This was a danger—a mistake. You did not find the woman of your dreams in Vegas of all places.

But what if I had?

* * *

Four days later, we were in my room, her back pressed against the door, my lips on hers, and I panted, trying to catch my breath.

"Kendall. We need to take a break."

"I'm not a virgin, Evan," she whispered, and I just shook my head, cupping her face.

"That's not why. However, we have a wedding to make it to, and I don't think I can fuck you hard against this door quick enough for us to make it on time."

Her eyes widened, and then she grinned. "After the wedding then?"

"After the wedding, we're not going to get out of that damn bed. Or that shower. I promise." I reached around, cupped her ass, and she groaned.

"That sounds like a plan to me."

"And Kendall? When we get back home? I'm not letting you go either."

This time, I meant to say the words to test them out for myself.

And when she smiled, she cupped my face. "When you get home, I'm not letting you go. Except for deployment. Then I'll have to watch you go." She swallowed hard, and we both were thinking of the fact that as soon as I got back, we had two weeks before I headed out to Afghanistan with the rest of my squadron.

I pressed my forehead to hers and let out a deep breath. "We'll jump that bridge when we get to it."

"That's not the saying," she teased.

"No, but we'll figure it out."

Because we had to. A connection like this didn't come often, and I'd be damned if I'd miss out on it because of fate, jobs, or circumstances.

By the time we made it to the chapel, all of us were a little buzzed from energy and the tequila shots we had done beforehand.

I gripped her hand tightly, looked at Kendall, and knew that she was the one. But I needed to stop, hold back, and tell myself that this was stupid. That we didn't need to do anything too spontaneous right then.

And as Keegan and Lacey vowed to love each other forever, as the Cher impersonator told us that we didn't need to turn back time because this was the time that we were living in for now and forever, I looked at Kendall, and I didn't want to say goodbye.

"Marry me."

Kendall's eyes widened. "Evan. Are you serious?"

"Dude. For real?" Keegan asked.

"Fuck yeah!" Ward shouted.

Britney and Lacey spoke at the same time, their words coming so quickly I could barely hear.

But all I could do was look at Kendall.

Look at her and wait for her answer.

"I know this is insane. I know this makes no sense. But I *feel* this, Kendall. You do, too. This connection doesn't come often. Let's not lose this chance at what we could have."

"Aww," Lacey whispered as Britney shushed her.

"You're crazy," Kendall blurted, and my heart fell before she threw her arms around my neck. "But fuck yeah, so am I. yes, I'll marry you."

The next day, completely sober yet caught up in the moment, I vowed I would love Kendall forever. That I would be her protector. That she would be mine.

And I knew that this might have been quick, but it wasn't a mistake.

She was mine.

And now I had a chance to earn her.

. . .

Two years later.

The Humvee shook on the gravel road, and I held onto the bar, trying not to throw up.

I was nauseous from being car sick, something I had never had an issue with until recently. But the concussion I had gotten last year when the IED had hit made things a little more complicated now. We were going to the next space, prepping for when the commanders told us it was time to go out.

We were the Air Force Pararescue. It was our job to always be in the thick of it.

One of my men was driving, Ward next to him, Keegan next to me.

We had two more weeks out here, and then we could go home to our wives.

To Lacey, Britney, and Kendall.

The women that we had married in a slight rush but fought for. Things weren't easy. And I knew that they were harder on the girls in some aspects, but the six of us were stationed at the same base and working our asses off to make things work.

Keegan sighed into his mic. "I can't believe I can finally meet my kid,"

I just shook my head at my friend. "I can't believe you haven't met the newborn yet."

"At least I was there for the birth of our first one. I just hate that we missed the second."

"I'm surprised I could even make it in time to be there for the birth of ours," Ward said from the front, and that familiar twist in my gut came back in full force.

Kendall and I were waiting since we hadn't waited for anything else, and getting married quickly, when your husband was constantly out of the country, hadn't been easy for our marriage, but we were making it work. I loved her more than life, and I wasn't going to change a damn thing.

I should've thought better about that. I should've remembered that life burned, but it also was frail.

So when the explosion came, the shouts were quick, the grunts loud.

Later I would remember the glass shattering against me, metal screeching, the heat, and inferno.

Our driver, Jake, screamed for his mother, and then there was nothing, and I opened my eyes, blood pouring from a wound on my head, having been thrown from the Humvee.

Jake was gone. I could see it in the angle of his neck. The rest of our squadron came out to protect us, to make sure that whoever had taken out our Humvee wouldn't come back with a second wave.

There were shouts and screams, and I tried not to throw up, tried not to scream. Instead, I moved towards the two men that had been my everything, had been my brothers in all but blood, at their vacant gazes, and I knew that there was no going back.

The blood became sticky on my face and I could no longer fully recognize Keegan or Ward through the haze.

I knew one thing.

They had made their wives widows, and I refused to do the same.

Chapter Two

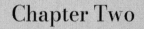

Kendall

S team blasted into my face, and I sighed happily, the scent of chicken and lemon and herbs filling my nostrils. I tossed the contents of my wok with one hand while checking the rice cooker with my other.

I enjoyed making a different kind of stir-fry for this evening's dinner at the inn, something I didn't always get to do in a place where its residents tended to like barbecue and steak more than anything. But I was always allowed to do whatever I wanted with my menu, which included a special of the day, which was this stir-fry. I got to use vegetables, play to my strengths, including sauces, and just have fun.

The entire kitchen smelled of garlic, soy sauce, and sesame oil. And my stomach grumbled.

"I'm working on the steaks, *chef*, are you set?" The man behind me grumbled, and I grit my teeth

Because the way he said *chef* wasn't polite or respectful. No, he did not like me.

"We're all set, Roger. Begin plating, and I'll come in after you."

"I can do this, *chef*," Roger snapped, and I gave him a look before he shrugged and did as I told.

Sandy, my sous chef, came forward, eyes narrowed at Roger's back before she took a look over my station for me. "I've got this in case you want to go handle that," she muttered under her breath.

I rolled my eyes before letting her do the finishing touches. "Thanks, Sandy."

I winked as I said it, the humor in my eyes real. Because I liked Sandy, she held the fort down at Wilder Resort and Winery when I had needed to learn the kitchen. When the previous chef had abruptly quit, the second or third in the long line of chefs who hadn't wanted to work for the Wilder brothers, Sandy had done her best, though she only worked part-time because she wanted to spend time with her children.

I respected Sandy's decision and knew she was a fantastic chef who could easily have my job if she wanted. She just didn't want it.

Knowing exactly where you stood and what things you wanted were admirable, and sometimes I felt like I didn't live up to that.

I went to stand beside Roger, finishing up the plating, as Roger gently trailed his finger down my arm.

I held back a shudder and told myself he was just doing it by accident as we were working in close quarters, but then he did it again.

I took a step to the side and narrowed my eyes at him. I wanted to get these plates out, and I didn't want to make a scene, and honestly, it was hard to tell with Roger since I knew he didn't like working for a woman and thought he could do better than I could. However, I was the head chef, and he could just deal with it.

I also didn't want him touching me.

The servers came in, took the final plates, and I went to work on a dessert when Roger tripped and gripped my ass.

I whirled on him, taking his wrists and using the moves that Evan had taught me all those years ago to take him down to the ground.

He let out a yelp and writhed underneath me as I pinned his arm to his back.

"If you ever touch me again, we're going to have problems." My pulse raced even as my ears rang from panic.

Roger's eyes widened in alarm, but I saw the sickly anger under it. "Do you see what she's doing? I'm on the floor, covered in grease, and she's abusing me. Call the police."

"I don't think so," Sandy growled, her hands on her hips.

"I saw what you did, and the cameras will have caught it, too."

"Fuck both of you."

"You know what, Roger? We don't need you. You're done."

"You can't fucking fire me. You're just the ex-wife who fucked one of the owners. You don't have the right to fire me."

"She does," a familiar voice growled from the doorway, and humiliation washed over me.

Of course, *he* would be the one who walked into my kitchen right at that moment. It didn't matter that there were five other Wilder brothers who could have seen this, who could have come and handled this. Hell, even Alexis, our wedding planner, and my friends could have come in here. Maddie, the tasting room and wine club manager—and one of my best friends—could have walked in here and seen this and helped.

But no, it had to be my ex-husband.

Evan goddamn Wilder.

"I have this, Evan."

"I can see that. What did he do?"

And it was words like that that made me hurt. Because it wasn't that he came in and wondered why I was shoving someone. No, Evan had to assume that it was for a reason. That I would do this because of some action. Because that was who Evan was. He would never think I'd attack without reason.

And I hated it. I hated that this man could just walk away from me so quickly.

"I didn't fucking do anything. This bitch just attacked me. Are you going to let this happen on your property? I thought you were a real man, Wilder."

"We don't have time for this, Roger. I'm going to let you go, and then you're going to calmly walk away from this property and never come back."

"You can't fire me. You don't have the authority," he reiterated.

"She does. This is her kitchen. In case you didn't get it through your thick skull, *you're fired.*"

"I didn't do anything!" Roger snapped as he scrambled

to his feet. I pulled back, ready for him, or at least trying to be, but he didn't move towards Sandy or me. Sandy, the calmest and most rational one of us all, continued to stir the sauce on the stove and work on our remaining orders.

"I have desserts to make, Roger. And you're done here."

"Your kitchen would be nothing without me," he snarled.

"Don't flatter yourself. You're mediocre at best, and the only thing you were good at was taking orders, and that quickly dissolved. And if you ever, *ever* put your hand on another woman in my sight? We'll have problems."

"You touched her?" Evan growled as he moved forward, his fists clenched at his side.

I moved in between them, not wanting to make a scene, and honestly, not wanting to be the chew toy in between them.

Because while Evan and I were divorced and hadn't seen each other for nearly eight years, we slept together last month, right in this kitchen prep area. I'd had to bleach the site numerous times just to get it out of my memory.

I didn't even remember exactly how it happened. Just, one minute we were screaming at each other, giving each other snide remarks, the next, his mouth was on mine, and my hand was on his dick.

Then Evan had walked away. He'd walked away and hadn't looked back because what we'd done had been a mistake.

I knew it. It had to be a mistake. Because I didn't get to have Evan Wilder. I hadn't been able to keep him before, so I wasn't going to get to now.

I wasn't going to be the person in the middle of his territorial pissing contest either.

"I've got this, Evan."

"Oh, so now you don't want your little husband to take care of you?"

"Ex," I snapped, and I thought I saw Evan stiffen, but maybe I just imagined things. Because I needed to.

"You're done, Roger."

"We'll take care of it," Eli, Evan's older brother and my boss, said as he walked in.

"Evan, why don't you take care of something at the winery. I'm sure they need you there since you're the boss and all."

"What the fuck did this bastard do?" Evan asked, ignoring everyone but me.

I sighed. "He touched my ass. Again. And I don't stand for that. If we have a problem, you need to tell me now."

"You asshole," Evan growled, moving forward, but then Eli was there, pulling his brother back.

"Evan, stand down. Roger? You're going to come with me."

"Fuck you."

"That's just fine. But you're going to have to handle the Wilders now."

"I was handling it just fine."

Eli gave me a tight nod. "You're a Wilder, too. We take care of our own."

I knew my former brother-in-law hadn't meant to hurt me with that, but I was a Wilder still. I hadn't changed my name back, and I told myself it was just because of the paperwork. But no, it was for something far more annoying.

I missed the stupid asshole who I didn't love anymore, because I couldn't.

I raised my chin, trying to hold it together. "I have to get back to work. Thank you for taking him out of here."

"Bitch," Roger muttered under his breath before he stomped out, Eli following, after he gave me a look.

Evan still stood there, not having listened to anyone and leaving as asked.

"Kendall."

My name on his lips hurt. As it always did.

I looked at him then, at his dark black hair that was

too long. It covered his face now, and as he roughly pulled it back, I saw the muscles in his arms work, the way that his blue eyes narrowed at me.

I wanted to hate him. I needed to hate him.

And the fact that I couldn't told me I shouldn't have taken this job. But it was the best one that I had ever had, and I loved it here.

I just hated him.

"I have to get back to work. I have desserts to make, and I've already made enough of a scene."

"Kendall."

"Go away, Evan."

He just stood there, and I waved him away before I went back to desserts, since Sandy and I had to take up the rest of the slack from Roger. We needed a third person during the major rush, but we were at the end of it now, and so when I noticed Evan finally leaving, my shoulders relaxed marginally.

"He grabbed my ass once, too."

I looked at Sandy, and my eyes widened. "You didn't say anything, Sandy. You should have told me. I'm so damn sorry."

"I thought it was an accident. I'm sorry. Next time somebody comes and touches me like that, I'll tell you."

"And I damn well better notice in the first place. I'm

so sorry. You shouldn't have to work in a situation like that. You should tell Eli."

"I will after we finish this. And you should go take a breath. You haven't even had a glass of water since we started for the day. We're almost done. Just breathe."

I shook my head. "No. I've got this."

"I've got this too, Kendall. Go splash water on your face or something."

"I thought I was the boss here," I teased. My hands were clammy, and I was indeed shaking. Maybe I did need that moment.

"Go. You've trained me well. I've got this for now."

I looked at her then, wiped my hands on my apron, and nodded tightly.

"I'm just going to take a breather. I'll be right back."

"We're on time. We're good." Sandy gave me a small smile, and I squeezed her hand before I went outside to take a breath.

We were outside San Antonio, in the Hill Country, though not as far west as Fredericksburg. So while we couldn't see the city's lights, it was still decently bright out here, thanks to the inn itself.

The air was cool, and I was grateful for the slight cold front that had come through, just so I could breathe. My cheeks were red, and it had nothing to do with the steam that had flashed in my face earlier.

31

No, it was all embarrassment. Because I had let Roger stay for too long, thinking I could handle it, and instead he had dared to hurt my friend and coworker. What else had he done when I had been trying to be the boss?

This was the first time I was in this position, to have this much power and responsibility. I only had the Wilders to answer to.

I thought I could handle this, but now I wasn't so sure. Because someone who could deal with everything that came with being head chef wouldn't have let Sandy get hurt. No, instead, I had made an embarrassment of myself and a mess of everything.

All because I thought I could handle Roger on my own.

And it had taken the Wilders to get him out of the kitchen when I couldn't. Yes, I had taken him to the ground and stood up for myself, but it hadn't been enough.

I was just so tired of not being enough.

I ran my hand over my face and then took a sip of the bottled water I had brought out with me.

"Are you okay?"

I stiffened, my shoulders tightening at the sound of his voice.

Why did he always have to find me at my worst?

"I need a minute alone, Evan. Just give me that."

"I'm asking if you're okay. Do you need to talk with someone?"

I looked at him then. The anger in his eyes had dimmed somewhat. Now he looked worried and perhaps as tired as I felt.

"I just want a moment alone. I don't need to talk to anyone. I don't need you to handle this. I just want to breathe."

"I can get Alexis out here if you're maybe mad at me? Just tell me."

"Why can't you just listen to me? For once in your goddamn life, just listen to me, Evan. I need a moment to think."

"And I'll give you that. I just need to make sure you're okay."

"And you aren't listening to my wishes. You don't get to do this. You don't get to walk into my life over and over again and just take over. I don't want you here, Evan. The only reason I took this job is because it's the best place for me, despite the fact that you're here."

It looked like my words had struck a mark because his face paled, but he narrowed his gaze at me. "I get to do this. We work under the same goddamn roof. We can be civil."

Rage erupted. "You're not my husband. You decided

that. You're the one who walked away, so why don't you do it the fuck again?"

"Because you were hurt? I'm not just going to walk away when some man had his hands on you."

"It doesn't matter if anyone has their hands on me. It is not your right to care."

"As your fucking boss, it's my right."

"You're not my boss. We've already discussed this. Eli is my boss. You are just a sad attachment that I have to deal with every time that I see you."

I hated the words spewing from my mouth. I hated how full of vitriol they were. Because I couldn't hate him, and that was the goddamn problem. I couldn't be this angry or this rude. But I had to be strong. Because every time I saw Evan, I just wanted to go to my knees and weep and ask him why he left me. Why I wasn't good enough.

"Kendall."

"Roger didn't hurt me. He pissed me off and bruised my pride. It won't be a problem. But you need to go. You don't get to handle my problems. You didn't handle them before, and you won't goddamn do it now. You don't get to do it with your fists or your words. You don't get to do anything."

"Kendall. I can't just walk away."

I threw my head back and laughed, the sound so

painful I nearly cried. "That's rich. I don't care. Evan. We're not married anymore. Yes, we fucked, but that didn't mean anything, am I right?" I asked, each word a blow to my own heart. It wasn't making love. It had been just sex. It'd been a hard fuck against a metal table that hadn't meant anything to him. He had walked away yet again.

"You're the one who let me, *again*," he snarled, angry now.

I let the blow hit, a slash against my heart once, twice, and then a thousand more times.

Had I let him walk away? Or fuck me? Which one was he talking about?

I didn't care. I *couldn't*. Even though all I wanted was to care.

"Go away, Evan. I don't want to do this. I can't do this. You were right before. Having sex again after all these years was a mistake. Blame it on our hormones or a long fucking day. I don't care. But it's over. It was over a long time ago, you saw to that. So I cannot do this, Evan. I still carry your goddamn name, and I can't hide from it. I work with your family, nearly your *entire* damn family, and I can't walk away from it. But I love this job, and you being here isn't going to ruin this for me. For once, I'm making something for myself. That has nothing to do with you other than you're here. And I can't get rid of your presence, but I can ask you, beg you, to just stay away."

He looked at me then, and I still couldn't read him. "I don't want you to hate me."

If he only knew.

"We can't always get what we want. Isn't that the saying? The song? I don't know anymore. But you don't get to come at me like this. Just go away." I let out a shaky breath and stared him right in the face. My chin raised because it was the only thing I could do. "I'm going to date again, Evan. I have. And I will again. And if I get into trouble, if something happens, if I'm hurt, you don't get to be the one that fixes it. I will do it. My friends will do it." I didn't mention my family; there was no use lying to him there because he knew that truth. "You don't get to be part of anything in my life. You made that decision, and now you get to live with it, and you get to respect my choices for once. Don't talk to me again. I'm done. We don't get to be friends. We don't get to be coworkers. We get to be *nothing*. Because you made that decision before, and now we're both going to finally live with it. Don't try to fix my problems again, Evan. I don't need you. And you clearly never needed me."

And before he could say anything, I turned and walked away from him, back into the kitchen, past

Sandy and our other two assistants, and walked right into the fridge. I closed up behind me, the cool air shocking at first, then calming.

And then I put my face in my hands, and I wept.

Once again, I was crying over a Wilder.

And I wasn't sure how much more I could take.

Chapter Three

Evan

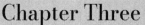

The explosion shot me off my feet, and I landed in a heap, the action so fast I didn't even have time to scream. I tried to get up, only when I looked down, all I saw was blood. Blood and smoke and gore and whatever the hell else there was.

I looked around at my men, tried to crawl to them, only I couldn't say anything, couldn't do anything.

People were screaming, shouting orders, bullets spraying over us. This was war. It wasn't pretty. It wasn't in a movie where the good guys won.

This was me lying and dying in a field, trying to find the rest of my leg.

Someone was over me, shouting orders, and when they put their hand on my thigh, as they gripped my thigh, trying to stop the blood, pain lanced through my remaining limb, slamming into me, and I turned to the side and vomited. Still, as I tried to lean up, to figure out what the hell was going on, the dream, because it had to be a dream, shifted once again.

This time I was back in the Humvee, Keegan and Ward laughing at something our driver was saying.

Why couldn't I remember the kid's name? I had been to that kid's funeral. I knew that kid. Yet I could only think of Keegan and Ward.

I wanted to yell, to say get off the road, take another way. But the IED was right ahead of us, and I was going to be the only one that made it out alive.

I ended up with my second concussion from that. I knew this. I hadn't lost my leg this day. No, it had been another explosion that had done that. An explosion and array of bullets had sliced through my flesh as if they were a hot knife in butter.

And I couldn't stop it. I couldn't stop any of them.

"What's wrong?" Ward asked, frowning at me.

"We have to get out of here. We have to stop."

But they weren't listening to me. Why weren't they listening to me?

They both looked at me then, blood beginning to seep from the wounds on their faces as if I was watching life end in real time in the most horrific of ways.

I screamed again, and then it went away, and I was standing at the doorway of Lacey's house as she ran to me and wrapped her arm around my shoulders.

"I'm so sorry. I'm so sorry."

Why was she telling me she was sorry?

It should've been me. It should've been me telling her I was sorry. That I hadn't found a way to save our friends.

And then Britney was holding me, too, both of them leaning into me as they sobbed, kids wailing, tears seeping into my clothes.

I couldn't do anything. I could just stand back and watch as my friend's widows realized that their lives had been changed forever.

And then I turned in the dream, saw Kendall standing there, a frown on her face as she looked down at her hands.

Blood drenched them, and she looked up at me, then down at her hands again, and slowly slid the wedding ring off, the clink of white gold and the tiny diamond hitting the pavement with such a loud clang, it echoed within my dreams.

"We didn't fight. We never fought."

"Kendall!" I screamed, wanting her to take back the words.

And then the explosion hit again, but it wasn't me.

No, it was her.

And I looked down at my own hands, coated in blood, and screamed.

I sat up from the dream, pissed off at myself for not being able to wake up from it on my own. I was usually better than that, but the fight with Kendall seemed to have stuck me in that dream that I couldn't get out of.

Not that I could blame her. I was the fuckface who had left her. And now was forced to work with her because she was so damn good at her job.

But I couldn't fix it.

I couldn't fix her.

And I was stuck here.

Sweat slicked my body, and I cursed at myself again for not being able to wake up from that dream. I should be better at this by now because it wasn't as if nightmares were new for me. This was my normal, and yet I hadn't been able to get out from this one. However, the twist on this one had been slightly different. The wedding ring and the mix of all of my fears into one

41

seemed to be amplified. I just needed to add part of the dream where one of my brothers got killed in front of me, or a bomb hit the Wilder Resort, and would be a trifecta of everything that hurt.

I sighed and slowly worked to get out of bed, reaching for my prosthesis, making sure it was a secure fit. Technology had changed dramatically since I had first lost my leg. I didn't have the same fitting or pain issues that I had in the past, and I was grateful for that. Some of my friends down at the VA had been dealing with prosthetic problems for over a decade now, sometimes longer, to the point that they'd had to exclusively use a wheelchair when they hadn't been able to get it fitted correctly.

But I didn't have that problem as much anymore. Even through the VA, my doctors were fantastic and I was lucky to be where I was. San Antonio had a large retired Air Force contingent, as well as other military services because of all the bases around here. It was a good place to retire, even when retiring from the military after twenty years mostly meant you were in your thirties, ready to start a new life and a new job.

That was how it had been for my family and me. We were all relatively young, starting over even though I knew each of us, even my youngest brother, all felt older beyond our years. But we were figuring out our paths. All thanks to Eli.

He had been the one to find this land and this inn and somehow convinced us all to join him in this near folly. I couldn't believe that I had said yes to helping run a fucking winery.

Our uncles had owned a winery in Napa years ago and had taught me everything they knew before they had passed, and the money that we had gotten from their will had helped buy this place, but I still felt out of my depth more often than not. I was grateful to Edmond and Edward for teaching me what I needed to know.

Without them, I didn't know what I'd be doing or where I would be.

I was okay at finding my path.

Even if, somehow, I was a Winery Director.

I was glad that most of the people from the previous owners had stayed on, because they were the true masters who knew what they were doing in terms of making wine. My job was to organize them, along with my brother, Elijah. Everyone else worked at the inn part of the resort, but Elijah and I were part of the winery. It felt good to do something and have it matter, even if it wasn't saving the world.

I showered, got ready for the day, and grumbled my way to coffee and out of my cabin. Elijah was already there, the golf cart running and a grin on his face. "I'm hyped up on coffee. Let's go."

"Why are you here?" I asked, snarling. I wasn't sure I was in the mood for Elijah's perky attitude right then.

"I'm here because I have the golf cart, and I want to get you to work."

"What if I wanted to walk? For a workout?"

"Just get in the damn golf cart," he grumbled, his smile slipping before he slicked his hands down his nice suit.

I was wearing jeans and an old gray Henley, one that fitted to my muscles according to one of the guests that had come in, but I didn't care. Elijah liked his suits because they were far different from what he wore when he was on active duty and now wanted to feel like a new man. Plus, he was the operations director for the winery. Suits worked for him.

I was just the one who was the head of the winery and grumbled in the background.

"How was your date with Joy?" I asked as I levered myself into the golf cart.

"She's fucking amazing." Elijah grinned at me, and I shook my head, wondering why I'd even asked.

"Is she the reason why you're so hyper?"

"I told you it was the coffee, but that was because I stayed up way too late." He winked, and I just groaned.

"I don't want to know about your sex life."

"I'm not telling you about my sex life. Yes, we did have sex, but it was more of us just talking all night. She's amazing, Evan. I mean, she just gets me. I really like her."

That was a change. So far, the only person in a serious relationship of my siblings down here in Texas was Eli. Eli and Alexis were getting married soon and moving in together. Our baby sister Eliza was up in Colorado, married, and a mom.

I had been the first one of us who had gotten married, but I was divorced and now forced to work with my ex-wife.

But Elijah sounded serious. That was something.

"So, are we going to meet this Joy?" I asked as we turned down the path, and Elijah nodded and waved at a few guests. I just folded my arms over my chest and tried not to glare. I needed to not hurt this family company. It was nice to work with my brothers after so long of us being separate. But now, I felt like if I didn't act calm and rational, I would be the one that hurt my family. And I didn't want to be that person. They all worried about me enough. I didn't want it to be any worse.

I knew each of my brothers had their own issues for why they had gotten out of the military. Each of us were either forced out of it or left because things just didn't work.

Elijah tapped his fingers along the wheel. "I don't know. Meeting with the Wilders is a bit of a thing."

I raised a brow as I stared at him and shook my head. "We just threw Alexis to the wolves with Eli, didn't we?"

Elijah shrugged. "Pretty much. But she works with us, so it's not the same thing."

That just reminded me of Kendall, and I held back a sigh.

"I heard about what happened with Kendall. You want to talk about it?"

My stomach clenched. "Do I look like I want to fucking talk about it?"

"No, but you never want to talk about her, and I feel like you should, so maybe this time is different."

"I'm not going to talk about Kendall. There's no need. She's not my wife anymore, and she can clearly take care of herself."

We got out of the golf cart, and Elijah just sighed.

"My situation isn't yours. You should have Joy meet us," I said after a minute.

"Maybe. Before you guys find a way to scare her away, I can have you guys controlled and ready."

"As long as Joy makes you happy, go for it."

My brother gave me a long look. "I'm surprised you didn't make the whole joke of Joy bringing me joy."

We walked through the winery entry area, nodded at a few of the workers, and I shook my head. "I thought about it, but I thought it was idiotic."

"Well, just don't do it around her. She hates that."

"Honestly, I would hate it, too."

Maddie came up to us then, her smile tight, and I had a feeling she had heard Elijah talking about Joy. I knew that Maddie had a crush on Elijah, but I was doing my best to studiously ignore it. I wasn't even sure Elijah even realized, since he was dense about certain things like that.

"Hello boys, I see you've already had your coffee," she said as she pointed at Elijah, then handed me a cup. "Here you go, Evan."

My brows rose. "You don't have to get me coffee, Maddie."

"Well, I have bad news about the wine club, so I'm trying to butter you up with caffeine." She took the spare cup that I had a feeling was supposed to go to Elijah and took a sip herself.

"What's the bad news?" Elijah asked as I tensed.

"Two words." Maddie cringed.

"Dodge Ranch," I growled.

Dodge was the resort on the other side of town, and

for some reason, they hated us. It was a family-run establishment like ours and a little more rundown, but they did their best to try to steal our clients and make us look like shit. When we'd had vandalism in the past, we had gone so far to think it was Dodge or one of his sons, LJ or Brayden. In the end, it had been someone else, but I still didn't trust the family.

"Talk to me," Elijah said as he and Maddie moved off, leaving me to work with my vintner and vineyard manager.

I didn't work the grapes, nor was I the cellar master or someone who actually made the wine. My job was to direct it all, to put people in the right places, and Elijah was in charge of operating the sales, PR, and tasting room.

We had two separate entities of a larger branch, all part of the main Wilders. It was complicated, but we liked complicated. And it was completely different from what we used to do.

I went to speak with our winemaker, aka the vintner, and went over the next cab and red blend that we were going to be tasting soon.

There was a frost coming in according to the weather alert, but that could change at any minute. South Texas weather made no sense to me. Then again, neither did most weather these days. It was in the seventies right now, and the fact that people were talking about frost just confused me.

A wine tour was going on, and a couple of women gave me a look from head to toe, and I just shook my head.

"I see the Wilders never disappoint," Jay, my wine-maker said, and I rolled my eyes.

"Apparently, we are also on the tasting menu," I mumbled, surprising myself, and Jay just grinned.

As the tour came over, I nodded at my tour guide and answered any questions that I could, though Jay was far more knowledgeable than me. He was the one practically teaching me, and I was always learning.

Sometimes it felt like that, at least.

As the tour started to move away, two of the women with dark hair, wide grins, and tight leggings stayed.

"So, you're one of the Wilders?" one of the women asked, and I nodded. I needed not to be an asshole and push these women away.

"I am. Are there any questions I can answer for you? I don't want you to miss your tour."

"Oh no, we'll keep up. We were just wondering if you'd like to come with us to the rest of the tasting? I know it's a bit early for wine, but you work here after all."

I shook my head. "Don't worry, ladies. You'll have fun because we do mimosas with our sparkling tasting."

"Oh, we're excited."

Out of the corner of my eye, I saw Maddie and Kendall walk by, Kendall's shoulders tight, and I held back a curse. Well, if she was going to start dating, why shouldn't I?

It had been eight years, and I hadn't had a serious relationship, but I'd been with women. It wasn't like I could say no to everything. But, as the woman in front of me grinned at me, asking me once again if I wanted to join them, I knew I couldn't.

Even if Kendall thought I would, I wasn't in the mood to date someone who would ask me out at work. Nor was I in the mood to deal with anyone else, other than my own emotions or feelings.

Because frankly, I didn't want to deal with those either. And that dream still haunted me, so I shook my head again.

"No can do, ladies. I'm a little busy, but our tour guides will take care of you, don't worry."

The tour guide, Josie, raised her brows and grinned. "Come on, ladies, make sure you catch up. We don't want you to get lost in the barrels."

"That might be fun," one of the women purred, but

then she shrugged and walked away with her friend, and I rolled my shoulders back and went back to work.

I was done. Just done.

My day had already started off like shit, and as Kendall glared at me, walking down the path with Maddie again, I knew it wasn't going to get any better.

I needed to get my act together, to do better for my family.

And that meant getting over my ex-wife.

Finally.

Chapter Four

Kendall

My alarm shrilled, but I was already awake. It was hard to sleep these days, even when exhaustion set in when my mind kept whirling with a thousand different thoughts.

I rolled over to the edge of my bed, turned off the alarm on my phone, and sat up, stretching.

I still needed to move a few boxes from my guest room into here and unpack them, as there was barely anything on my walls, and I hadn't changed the paint color since I moved in. Everything was a whisker gray, builders gray, and nothing spoke to me, but it was mine.

When I worked at the restaurant downtown, I had worked underneath a Michelin Star chef and learned so much. It was because of him I was the chef I was today, but being in the kitchen meant notoriously long hours and no real time for life outside of food and the drama and politics that came with the kitchen full of steam and sharp utensils.

My house barely felt like my own because I was rarely in it. I worked hard for my small home. I was the one who paid the down payment, and the mortgage was in my name. Nothing to do with this place had anything to do with my family or the Wilders. Except for now, whatever the Wilders paid me went towards that mortgage.

I was rarely home these days, even with running my own kitchen.

There had been no place for me to grow at that beautiful restaurant that I used to work at. The other person at my level was related to the chef. It was a family-run restaurant, and yes, it sucked that I wasn't even going to be considered for a promotion, but in the end, my counterpart was brilliant. Talented. They probably would have gotten it without the fact that they were related.

And so I had walked away as soon as I got the job at the Wilder's place. There had been rumblings that they were looking for a new chef for over a year, but I hadn't allowed myself to believe I was strong enough to be that person.

But the Wilders had goals, dreams they always had. There was no changing that. They worked hard and played hard, but were strong for each other.

Maybe not for me, but enough that it made sense that they worked as a unit.

So, when they were finally looking for that last chef, I tossed my hat in and tried.

And now I worked for them, and my ex-husband.

I gritted my teeth, got out of bed, padded my way to my bathroom, and got ready for my day.

Maybe I needed a cat. Of course, I wasn't home enough for a cat, but my house was lonely. I didn't even have any rugs on the floors, and though there was Texas heat, the Texas chill with its cold humidity still burned.

I loved my gray floors, but perhaps I could add a thick white shag rug underneath the bed where I could warm my toes once I got out of bed.

A cat wouldn't appreciate that, so again, it was good I didn't have one. Even if I wanted the company.

I showered, blow-dried my hair, pulled it away from my face—knowing I would put it in a braid later—and did the minimum amount of makeup. The heat in the kitchen would melt it right off, but I also wanted to look decent. Not for Evan. No, never for Evan, but for myself. I liked feeling pretty, and I rarely had occasion to do so these days. Thankfully, Alexis and Maddie, and sometimes our innkeeper Naomi, made me get all dressed up for dinner and drinks out, or even at the winery itself. But other than them, I didn't have much call for looking nice, so I did my best to look decent for myself. And Sandy.

I gritted my teeth, remembering that now that one of my assistant chefs was gone, fired and hopefully never coming back, I had to find someone to replace him.

Because while Sandy and I, as well as the rest of our kitchen staff, could handle nearly everything when we got swamped on weekends nights and during Sunday brunch, we still needed that help.

That meant I needed to find a talented chef that wasn't handsy and didn't make me want to throw them off the roof.

I went to my kitchen, made myself a coffee, and diced up some fruits for a fruit salad with toast. I made the bread that weekend, needing to relax, and baking soothed me. I had also made and salted my own butter, trying out new ways to fill my time. Not that I had much of it.

I was just taking a bite of my toast when my phone buzzed, and I looked down at it and steeled myself.

"Hi, Mom,' I said, trying to sound positive. There wasn't much positive for that.

"Kendall. Are you not at work? I assumed you would be at work."

Then why were you calling me if you thought I was at work? Of course, I didn't actually ask that because I didn't want the whole spiel, so I just let her go on.

"I'm going in soon. I work late nights, remember? Sandy does breakfast." That was so Sandy could do her best to have dinner at home with her family. I was the one who closed the kitchen and did the morning inventory too. Sandy could usually handle breakfast independently with our staff, and sometimes I joined in. Today was my late morning.

Not that watching the sunrise was late.

"I see." I ignored the ice in my mother's voice because she *didn't* see and would never be able to understand.

"How is everything?"

"I don't even know why you're asking me that. How could you ask me that?"

I sighed and sank down onto the chair at my kitchen island.

My mother began to drone on about work, her family, and everyone from the cashier at the grocery store to the barista who had gotten her order wrong.

Nothing was ever good enough for my mother.

I was on the top of that list of things that were never good enough but, after three decades of being that way, it was something I was used to.

"And don't even get me started on your father."

I rolled my eyes and muted myself, so I could finish my toast and she wouldn't hear the crunching. It wasn't like she needed my answers to any of her questions. She would just answer them herself.

I looked around at my kitchen and figured out what next update I wanted to do. Maybe I could ask East to help me out because I wanted to change out my faucet, get something a little grander in rose gold that seemed to be in all of those videos I watched online when I took a break. Do it yourself was great when you could actually do it yourself. But East Wilder was the maintenance director and handyman of the Wilders and knew what he was doing. He could probably help me with the kitchen sink.

"Now back to your father," Mother continued, and I unmuted it so I could hum along, and she would know I was actually somewhat paying attention.

"He's with that woman."

I crossed my eyes. I let out a breath. "I'm sorry, Mom."

"Oh, don't. Don't start. Let me tell you what he did."

And she proceeded to tell me what he did with his new wife.

That Vegas trip had been a change for nearly everyone in the family.

While I had met and fallen for Evan far too quickly and ended up married to him in a whirlwind romance, my parents had fought one too many times.

I was thankful I hadn't been part of it, and they wouldn't have cared if I was anyway. But after finding my father cheating for the fifth or so time in as many years, my mother had left my dad with a Vegas show-girl and had filed for divorce as soon as she returned home.

I was still in college, trying to deal with the fact that my new husband was getting deployed, and I was suddenly an Air Force wife, learning all the acronyms and other things that came with it, but I had put my all into it, trying to be a good wife. And I thought I had done so for the two years I had been with Evan.

On the other hand, my mother had put her effort in those two years to take as much from my father as she possibly could.

And frankly, I did not blame her. Not with the way that my father had cavorted around with women most of their marriage.

Now, Dad was on his second wife, which surprised

me since he had been with this one for a while now, and the Vegas showgirl was long since in the past.

Apparently, Mom and Dad had ended up at the same restaurant one night, even though they did their best to stay out of each other's orbits.

I thought it would have been easier if they had moved to different areas, but no, neither one of them wanted to leave. So, I was stuck being in the middle. Being in the middle and not really wanted. Someplace I was used to.

"I'm sorry, Mom."

"I just don't understand. I don't understand him. Much like I don't understand you. I hear you're working with Evan Wilder? Are you trying to get back with him? You know, Kendall, what happens when you try to get back with them? They just push you back more, and they lie, and they cheat."

I squeezed my eyes closed and let out a breath. "Evan didn't cheat on me. We just divorced." He never cheated on me. That much I knew. He was completely devoted to me until he wasn't. Until he left me high and dry, wondering what I had done wrong.

"Just don't you go back with him. And try to find someone else. What about that Dodge boy?"

I froze. "Excuse me?" How on earth did she know of the Dodges?

"I know his father, goes by Dodge. The owner of that resort. Such a lovely man."

Only my mother would think a narcissistic asshole who was trying to take down the Wilder's business would be a lovely man. But he had money, and that's what my mother liked. The man was married, though, and while I didn't know if he was a good man or not, my mother did not sleep with married men, not after what my father had done to her.

"I'm working, Mom. And I should probably head to work. I won't be dating anyone." Even though I told Evan I would be.

"You're getting older. You're nearly thirty now. When are you going to go out and actually be someone?"

I was thirty now, but I was pretty sure she had forgotten my last birthday, and the fact that I wasn't in my twenties. Of course, my mother routinely lied that she was in her forties, so maybe I was a teenager in her mind so that the math worked.

"I need to head out, but I'm glad we had this talk, Mom. It was good to hear from you." That was all pretty much lies, but I let them roll off my tongue.

"I will set you up if you don't say yes to that Dodge boy. LJ, I think it is. Or is it Brayden?"

I crossed my eyes and finally got my mom off the

phone before doing my dishes and sliding my feet into my shoes. I packed my bag, made sure I had my water and snacks and anything I needed, and said goodbye to my empty house, knowing it wouldn't be right if I got a cat. Who would ever be home to help take care of them? It wouldn't be me.

My phone rang again through my car as I pulled out onto the highway, and I answered, sighing.

"Hello, Dad."

"Did you hear what your mother did?" Dad asked.

He didn't wait for me to answer before he spewed about the restaurant and how my mother treated Josephine, my stepmother. My stepmother was only two years older than me, but I just let it go and listened to how my stepmother was amazing, sweet, and apparently vivacious, something I never needed to hear again, and how my mother was a shrew.

"I'm pulling into the Wilder's now. I need to get to work."

"You should go out with that Dodge boy. Dodge is a good man. He raised good sons."

"Goodbye, Father," I said as I hung up the phone, annoyed with myself for even answering. How on earth did they know that I had even spoken to LJ Dodge before? And how and why did both of my parents know and like the owner of the Dodge Ranch?

I got out of the car and pulled out my phone as it buzzed again, a tension headache right on its way.

My brother's name flashed on the screen, and I wanted to decline the call, but if I did, he would just find me. He always did.

"Hello, Kenny."

"Hey, baby sister. How are you?" He sounded high. Or at least too sweet. That meant he wanted something.

"I'm just heading into work now, so I don't have a lot of time to talk. I hope you're having a good day." I fought to make my voice calm, but it wasn't working.

"I know you're working. Working for the Wilder's now. I hear they have money."

Alarm bells started to ring and I swallowed hard. "I'm not sure what they have, but I'm working long hours to pay the bills. You know how it is."

He didn't know how it was, but it wasn't like I could say much.

"Anyway, the boys and I are heading back out to Vegas. You know Vegas. Big things happen there." He laughed at his own joke, even though I found nothing funny about it. Divorce and marriage in Vegas were rote these days.

"Have fun."

"I will have fun. But I'm going to need a couple.

Think you can do that? Spot your brother something? You know, just for the boys and me."

Bile filled my throat, but I swallowed it back as I leaned against the wall before I headed into the kitchen. I was so tired. Just so tired of this. Thankfully no one was around, everybody who worked there getting into their places, and the guests were on the other side of the building, but I was just so tired of this.

"I don't have money for you, Kenny."

"So you say. But you're doing so well. Working for the fucking Wilders? You've got money. Or at least you did when you were working for a decent chef."

"I've got to go, Kenny."

"Don't you dare hang up on me."

But I hung up on him and knew it would be a problem later.

I rubbed my temple and slid my phone into my pocket.

"Rough morning already?" a familiar and kind voice said as I looked up to see LJ Dodge walk into the hallway.

I stiffened for a moment and then reminded myself I liked LJ. He was nice. Yes, his brother and his father were assholes, and the company that they owned routinely tried to pull the rug out from the Wilders, but LJ wasn't that person. He didn't technically work for the family business and was constantly trying to mend fences.

I liked him, maybe not in the way that he wanted me to like him, but I did.

"Family. You know how it is."

His eyes tightened, and he gave me a small smile. "I know exactly how it is."

"Oh, you're not here for breakfast?" I asked, rolling my shoulders and trying to get back into the thick of things.

"Yes, actually. Meeting with a potential client." LJ had a law degree but also worked for his family's company.

My brows rose. "At the Wilder's?"

LJ winced. "It's nicer here. At least for the calmness where I don't have to introduce my father to everyone. But don't tell him I said that. I'm not in the mood for a lecture."

Considering I just got three lectures back-to-back-to-back, I understood.

"No problems, I won't say a thing. But you being back here means you might step into the space of a Wilder. You know that's dangerous."

I wasn't sure if the Wilder brothers hated LJ as much as they hated his brother and father, but there was contention there, and while I tried not to be in the middle of it, sometimes I was tossed there anyway.

"I'm well aware, and I'll do my best to stay out of their way. But I did come back here to ask you a question."

"I'm not sure what the special is because I let Sandy handle it this morning," I teased.

"Something with avocados, so I'm going to order it," he added, grinning.

"Sounds good to me."

"I'm here to see if you have an answer to that question I asked last week."

I stiffened, but his eyes were still kind.

"What question was that?" I asked, teasing. Teasing or flirting? I wasn't quite sure, but it felt different.

And I liked feeling different. Maybe that's what I needed to feel.

"I wanted to see if you wanted to go to dinner with me. I asked once, and you said you needed to think about it. Then I gave you space, so I'm asking again. Or perhaps I'm just continuing the question from the first. If you say no, I'll walk away right now, and I won't bother you again. I'm not that guy."

I nodded, knowing he wasn't that guy. He was nice. He wasn't a jerk.

And, as if I conjured the idea of what could go wrong from his question, from the corner of my eye, I saw Elijah and Evan walk by, both of them frowning as they looked over at us, before Elijah practically pulled Evan away.

I saw the anger and confusion in Evan's gaze, but I stamped down any worry. Because this was my life. LJ wasn't a bad person, he just had a bad family. And I knew exactly how that felt. I wasn't lucky like the Wilder's. I didn't have that connection. Neither did LJ.

And then I remembered that Evan had been asked out not once but four times in one day the day before, and I hadn't heard his answer because I hadn't wanted to know.

I told Evan I would start dating again, so maybe it's time I finally did that.

"Do you know what, LJ? Let's do dinner. But not at one of the resorts."

He grinned, his whole face brightening. "You're on. But you are the chef, so maybe I should let you pick the restaurant. I don't want to choose your rival or something."

I was truly afraid that my rival was in his family, but I ignored that feeling.

Just once, I wanted to be okay.

And so I was going to do this. I was going to go on a date. I was going to move on.

It had been eight years since he had walked away from me. Since Evan had left me as if I was trash and belongings he didn't care about.

I hadn't had an explanation then, and he didn't need an explanation from me now.

"I'll think of somewhere to go. But I'm excited, LJ. Really."

He grinned then, his whole face bright. "Good. We'll have fun, Kendall. I promise."

"I hope so. I'm looking forward to it."

I ignored the kernels of disappointment and loss within me, because they couldn't mean anything.

It was time to move on. From everything.

And everyone.

Chapter Five

Evan

Wine settled on my tongue and I opened my mouth, breathing in the air as I rolled the liquid over my tongue, the fruity with a hint of oak flavor intensifying.

"What do you think?" Jay asked as he took another sip of the blend we were currently tasting.

I frowned, concentrating. "I think you're a genius. It's exquisite. It opens up to the senses, not too heavy. It's a good blend for a weekly dinner drink that can be elevated to a special occasion depending on what's served with it."

Jay smiled at me, his eyes dancing. "Look at you, sounding like a true director."

I rolled my eyes. "You're the winemaker, the vintner. I'm just here trying to figure out the difference between a cab and a merlot."

Jay rolled his eyes. "As if you don't know the difference between a merlot and a blended cab. You knew that well before you moved here."

I shrugged and set down my tasting glass. "True. My uncles taught me well. And even though I do like beer, I am more of a wine man. Just don't tell my brothers."

Jay wrote a few notes down on the clipboard in front of him, both of us working on a few things at once. "I would hope your brothers would approve their winemaking director to actually like wine. Call me old-fashioned."

I ran my hand over my hair before I looked around the large building we were in, full of barrels, winemaking equipment, and countless team members who were good at what they did. We'd sunk our savings and livelihood into the inn and this business. This was all Wilder Wines, even if it didn't start out that way. "That's true. I like wine. I try not to drink every day, though, which is kind of hard for someone in the wine business."

"It's why we spit. Our little spit buckets make everything worth it," Jay said dryly.

I snorted. "Thanks for that. It's what we'll put on the brochures for Maddie. 'Don't worry, we spit.'"

"Well, if you wanted to make a sensual wine, spitting and swallowing could actually work for that," Jay added with a fake sneer.

I cringed, grateful I didn't have wine in my mouth just then. "I think we're going to have to hold off on that. Although, if you ask Maddie, she probably does have something in mind for a *particular* wine club."

"She's brilliant at what she does. I'm glad that she stayed on with the company when we switched owners. She's a talented tasting room and wine club manager. She does the work of two people and yet makes it seem like she can handle it all."

I frowned. "Can't she?"

"She can. And I joke that she's doing the work of two people. She's blended the jobs into one job, and she does have a team. You're not overworking your manager."

Relief flooded me. "Good. Though I would've thought Elijah would've noticed."

Jay gave me a look. "We are both aware that Elijah doesn't notice certain things about Maddie that he should, since they are obvious."

I winced. "Has he brought Joy around here yet?" I asked, keeping my voice low in case Maddie walked in. Although I was a little worried that I was even asking to begin with, considering that this was pure gossip at the workplace and not something I usually did. But I was having a day and avoiding thinking about the kitchen and Kendall. So whatever I had to do not to walk to that part of the property is what I would do.

"Joy hasn't been by when she's here. Thankfully. I don't think Elijah's doing that on purpose, though. I think it's just luck." Jay shook his head. "I don't know much more about it, so I guess I should stop gossiping."

I nodded tightly. "That's just what I was thinking. That's not something that we usually do."

Jay shrugged. "You're usually a little more closed off, a little growlier when we do our tastings, but you seem in a weird mood, so I kept going."

I shook my head. "Sorry if I'm being an asshole. I don't mean to be." I paused. "Okay, sometimes I mean to be. But not with you. You're good at what you do, Jay. You, Amos, and Maddie are the reason that we can even run this winery. You took on the Wilder brothers, and even though we have some knowledge of what we're doing, we don't have the inherent talent that you guys do. So, thank you."

Jay blushed. "I'm trying. You guys want what's best

for these wines, and while I understand that the former owners, as much as we love them, needed to retire for personal reasons, I'm glad you were the ones that bought them out. Some places would've just scrapped everything and started off from scratch."

I shook my head. "There's no way we could start from scratch. I don't know *that* much about wines."

"You know more than you think you do. I was just talking to my husband about that."

I frowned. "About what?"

"Matt was just talking about the different wines we had since I brought some home to taste. He was saying that word around the winery circles is that the Wilder brothers know their business. Even as of last year, you guys were an unknown commodity."

That honestly surprised me, since the winery was second seat to the inn, for good reasons. The inn kept us in the black and on the map. The wines were a bonus, and Elijah and I were perfectly fine with that. "Well, glad to know that we're on the winery tours' radar. We're not in Fredericksburg, though, so we're slightly off the beaten road."

"You are, but that's good. Because then you have your own center, and you're not competing with other winery tours. You guys have your own all-in-one here, and you work well with Roy up in the Austin area with their brewery."

"Us working together so that people can stay at either one of our resorts, and take the long drive to visit the other place for that tour, too, just sounded logical since we know each other."

"And not all wineries think to pair beer and wine."

"Not in the same day, mind you. We're not that crazy."

Jay grinned. "Good to know. Now, I guess I should get back to work. Maddie wants to meet with us for a few things."

"Don't mind me, I'll just follow along, and you tell me what to do."

"I'm pretty sure it's supposed to work the other way," Jay said with a laugh.

My phone buzzed, I looked down at the readout, and I quickly ignored it. The sight of Lacey's name sent a knife straight to my heart.

"Everything okay, boss?" Jay asked.

I nodded, keeping my face calm.

"Yes. Everything's fine. I'll deal with the call later."

Lacey would leave a message, and if it was an emergency, I would deal with it. Because I couldn't hear her voice just then, hers or Britney's. But I still helped them when I could. Because their husbands had asked it of me, and they would've done the same for Kendall if I had been the one who had died. Or if I had been the one who had stayed with her.

"If you're sure," Jay said, studying my face before we moved on.

Maddie came running into the room then, her face red, her hands shaking. For a moment, I thought that maybe my brother had been an idiot and had indeed brought Joy into the tasting room, then she held out a sticky note and growled.

"Dodge did it again. Fucking Dodge." Her voice shook, and the fact that she'd cursed at work nearly had me tripping over my feet. Not that Maddie didn't curse —she did—just not at work.

"Excuse me?" I asked, all thoughts of Maddie's crush on Elijah leaving my mind at the sound of that asshole's name.

"Dodge and Brayden once again screwed up our tour."

"How?" I asked, pulling the sticky note.

It just said. 'Fuck these guys' in big block lettering. I looked up at her, my mouth dropping. If possible, she blushed harder.

"I needed something to write down, and I couldn't think too hard as I got off the phone with Bliss."

It was as if ice shot down my system, and I looked at

her, praying that she was going to say something that wouldn't pull the rug out from beneath our feet.

"What did Bliss want?"

"They're having second thoughts."

The floor went out from beneath me, and I let out a deep breath.

While we had money, thanks to the sale of the winery in California from our uncles, we didn't have a full rolling amount of money to get us through the rest of our lives.

Yes, we did well, but we needed clients and clubs. Bliss had been one of the places we had gone to, with Elijah heading the call to help with the winery. Yes, we were a family business, but we needed a little bit more capital to keep going. The winery paid for itself, as did the resort, but we did have large clients to diversify our offerings. And Bliss was one of them. They had worked with us since the beginning, and while the company's president, the father of the Bliss brothers who helped run it, didn't like us too much, the next generation did. Like us, three brothers worked hard to keep the company working.

And now it seemed our rival Dodge and his dumbass sons were there to hurt us.

"What did they do?" I asked, biting out every word.

"Bliss has decided to possibly work with Dodge,"

Elijah growled as he came up from behind Maddie. My brother didn't notice the way that Maddie went even redder, her shoulders stiffening before she schooled her face completely, looking like the bright, bubbly blonde that she normally was, except for the bit of anger in her eyes.

I didn't think that anger had anything to do with Elijah just then since we all hated Dodge, but I wasn't one hundred percent sure.

"The Dodges are trying to take Bliss from us?" I asked, growling.

"Seems like it. Not quite sure what we're going to do about it, but we will do something." Elijah fixed his tie as Maddie began to pace beside me. Jay looked between us before someone called out his name, and he ran off with an apologetic look to help with one of the barrels.

"We're going to have to have a family meeting." I let out a breath. "We'll find something. Because fuck Dodge."

"Maybe Kendall can talk them out of this," Maddie mumbled to herself as she looked up from her phone and then froze.

Elijah and I turned to her and she paled, all blood leaching from her skin.

"Why would Kendall be able to help with this?" I asked, speaking slowly.

She sighed, looked between us, and then rolled her shoulders back.

"Because LJ and Kendall are friends. Something that you all know. LJ doesn't work for the company the way that Brayden does, but he still can try to steer them the right way. LJ's main job is a lawyer, even though he doesn't use his law degree as much as he used to with his family." She paused. "And, as you know, she has a date with LJ, so maybe they can talk about it then."

Rage filled me, and I fisted my hands at my side. "Kendall has a date with that mother fucker?" I asked, letting out a breath.

"We're at work, Evan. Please stop," she whispered, and Elijah stood by her side, glaring at me.

It wasn't lost on me that my brother was taking her side because, yes, I was growling like an untamed monster, but then again, I noticed Elijah tended to stand near Maddie as if wanting to protect her, though he didn't *see* her. But none of that was what was important just then.

"So, you are telling me that Kendall can try to convince LJ not to let his family take our business away because she's seeing him?"

"They're friends. I shouldn't have mentioned the date. It's none of your business, and I just betrayed my friend by even mentioning it. However, I don't know.

There needs to be something because I'm worried. Worried about what the Dodges want to do with this company."

I looked around as people were doing their best to ignore us, even though they were all listening in.

Elijah held up his hands as if realizing that at the same moment. "We can talk about this later."

"You guys can talk about it. I have someone to see," I snapped before I moved off.

"Evan, don't," Elijah called out, but I ignored him, even as Maddie began to talk quickly, trying to pull me back.

"Stop it, Evan. I shouldn't have said anything."

I held up my hand this time and moved away, stomping down the white stone path from the winery to the main building where the kitchen was. In the minutes it took to get there, I cooled down slightly, but then I saw her there, standing in the gardens, a small smile on her face as she looked down at her phone.

"Let me guess, LJ?" I asked, my hands shaking.

She looked at me and then around us, and I realized that we were alone. No one was in the garden except for us, so I moved closer.

"What do you want, Evan?"

"I hear you're going on a date with LJ. Our rival."

She stared at me for a moment in silence before she

let out a breath. "Oh, stop it. LJ isn't the rival. His brother and dad might be, but LJ's a good person."

"And so, what, you're just going to sleep with him to try to make him stay a good person?"

I should have expected the slap. She moved back, her eyes wide. She took a step back, looked down at her hand, then my face.

"Oh my God. I just hit you. I can't believe I did that. I'm sorry, Evan."

I shook my head and didn't bother rubbing my jaw since it didn't hurt. "You didn't hit hard, and I deserved it. I shouldn't have said that you were going to sleep with him to help the family."

Kendall still looked pale and like she was about to be sick. "I would *never*. I shouldn't have hit you. I am so sorry."

"It's fine. I said I deserved it. You should have hit harder."

Kendall seemed to want to say something but instead let out a breath. "Okay. But Evan, you don't get to say things like what you did about LJ to me. Ever."

"Then why are you going out on a date with LJ?"

"I can't believe Maddie told you, or was it Alexis?"

"Maddie let it slip because guess what? The Dodge family is trying to take away our business. They're taking the Bliss contract."

Kendall paled and shook her head. "What? LJ didn't mention that."

Why did that make me angrier? "Well, maybe you should talk to him."

"I'm not going to whore myself out for your family, Evan." Her face reddened, but I saw the hurt in her gaze. She should have hit me again.

"I didn't say that. I shouldn't have said anything to begin with."

"Then why are you here? Why are you yelling at me?"

"Why are you going on a date with him?" I barked.

"Because he's nice, Evan. Because he doesn't make me feel like *nothing*." Her eyes widened as she put her hand over her mouth before she turned away. "I have to go. I have work. But you don't get to do this. You don't get to care who I'm dating. You don't get to come at me. You don't get to make a scene."

I wanted to reach out, to apologize. Because I had deserved the slap. I had all but called her a whore, and I deserved it. I deserved that, and much more.

"Kendall."

I'm sorry.

"No. We don't do this. I'm sorry. I can't." She ran off and I let her, feeling like I had just been hit over and over, but by my own fist.

She should have hit me harder. She should have kept coming at me. Because I had hurt her.

I was just so tired. So tired of Dodge, of this with Kendall, the fact that we couldn't stop fighting with each other. I was just so tired of it all.

I sighed and turned, pissed off, and headed towards my cabin. I needed time to breathe, and then I would get back to work.

I turned, angry with myself, and tripped, not noticing the rock in the path. My prosthetic went one way, and I went the other, and I shouted, pain arching up my thigh as I lost my footing and hit the ground.

I looked at my betrayer, my leg that was no longer there, the one that I had lost because I hadn't been fast enough and just wanted to scream. To shout.

I was just so tired of all of this.

"Evan! Are you okay?"

Everett came out, running towards me. He tried to help me up and I pushed my younger brother away.

"I'm fine. Leave me alone."

"Of course, I'm not going to leave you alone. Here, let me help you up."

"*Just stop.*"

Everett glared at me, then handed me my prosthetic. I set myself inside it, and then he helped me stand up. "Are you okay?"

"I'm fine. Just leave me alone."

"I'm not going to leave you alone. You're my brother."

"You don't need to watch over me. I might have lost my leg, but I didn't lose my sanity. I can make it home by myself."

This time it looked like Everett had been the one who had been hit, and he took a step back.

"When you're done feeling sorry for yourself, we have a family meeting. And yes, Kendall will be there because she's a Wilder too. And she knows the Dodges. Don't treat her like shit, and don't treat us like shit just because you're not feeling well."

And then my brother left, and I stood there, shocked. Because Everett didn't lash out. He was the nice one. Yes, the TBI gave him headaches sometimes and messed with his moods, but he didn't normally lash out like that.

No, that was me, the bear with the thorn in his paw.

And I had just hurt my brother. Just like I had hurt Kendall. I'm probably just going to hurt anyone else on my path.

So I went home, limping the whole way, knowing I needed to rub my leg down, to make sure I didn't fuck up my prosthesis, and sighed.

Because I would be home. Alone. With nothing.

It was my own damn fault.

I needed to fix this. To apologize to my brother.

To do the same with Kendall.

And maybe, just maybe, figure out how to tell my ex-wife that I never stopped loving her.

And that, once again, I never deserved her.

Chapter Six

Kendall

In the past eight years, I had been on dates. I had even had, *gasp*, sex. It wasn't like I was still pining over my ex-husband. I was allowed to move on. And I had tried. But it had been nearly a year since I had been on an actual date. My lack of social life had nothing to do with Evan.

At least, that's what I told myself.

No, this had more to do with the idea that I didn't have time. Between my old job and getting prepared for the Wilders, I focused on my work. My career, my recipes. My kitchen was a damn good kitchen, and that meant I didn't get to go on dates. Not that I had been asked often, because I spent most of my time in my kitchen or in my house—which wasn't completely moved in yet even though I had been there for a couple of years.

I wasn't going to let myself think too hard on that, though.

That was why I stood in front of my long mirror tilted against my wall, a large purchase for me, but one that had made me happy with the wrought iron frame, and I tried to remember what I was supposed to wear.

It had to be something nice, since LJ had told me that we were going to Mahomes, a steakhouse right outside of downtown San Antonio. It was one of the best steakhouses in the city, and I needed to look nice. I was going to do my best.

That meant a little black dress, with a wrap that would cover my shoulders in case I got cold. At least, that's what I thought.

I sighed, shimmied out of my dress, then put on a different one that had capped sleeves, a heart neckline, and skimmed me at mid-thigh. Paired with a pair of black stilettos, I would look cute. Not too sexy and not too rundown.

I looked at my hair, ran my hands through it, and decided I would just leave it down.

I had blown it out, curled the ends, and figured if I put it up, I would be showcasing my neck and my cleavage a little too much, and I wasn't sure if I wanted LJ to focus on that this evening. It was our first date, and I didn't even know if a second one was an option.

LJ had asked me out a few times, and I'd finally said yes. Only, I wasn't sure it was because I wanted to go on a date with him, or if I just wanted to not think about Evan.

There was something seriously wrong with me.

I had already done most of my makeup, including my eyes. I just needed to finish with the mascara and pick a lip.

Was I going to go nude or red?

Considering the underwear I wore under this was sexy because if I wore anything like my granny panties or comfortable bra, you would be able to see the lines, I thought red might work. But I wasn't going for bombshell. And my eyes were already dark.

So a nude lip, with a little bit of gloss, and I would call it a day.

I sighed, annoyed with myself that I was focusing too hard on this.

This was a casual first date. I had been on first dates before. I didn't need to be so nervous.

And yet something in my stomach rolled, and I told

myself maybe it was just nerves. Nerves that wanted to escalate into something more.

I shook my head, put my phone, lip gloss, and other amenities in my tiny little purse, and figured that would be enough.

LJ had asked me out while I looked like crap, so I was going to count that as a win.

Right?

I went through everything again and made sure that the kitchen was doing fine, as Sandy texted me back. This was her one night to work for the week, and I smiled at her response.

Sandy: *Have fun. Don't worry about the kitchen. I've got you. We cook the filet well done, right?*

I laughed, I couldn't help it, sent her a kiss emoji, and gathered my things to head to the door.

The doorbell rang as soon as I got there, and I nearly tripped in my heels. I rolled my shoulders back, told myself I had this, and opened the door to see LJ standing there.

He was gorgeous, light brown hair with blond streaks that came from working hard outside in the sun. His hair was a little long on top and brushed back, so the waves in it made him look like a bronze god. He was tanned from working outside, too, rather than being sun-kissed from something fake. His hazel eyes were sparkling with a smile as they looked at me, and he wore nice slacks and a button-down shirt with a coat. He didn't wear a tie, and the button on his collar was undone. He looked casually elegant, and I didn't quite understand how he pulled that off.

"You look stunning, Kendall." I ducked my head, looked down at myself, and cringed. "Am I too dressed up?"

"No, you look just right. Seriously though, I feel like I should have worn a tie. Or brought you a corsage or something."

I looked at him then and snorted.

"No, I don't think we need to go the corsage route."

"I don't know. This does feel almost like a prom, doesn't it?"

I just shook my head and held my purse up. "Do I need a coat? I can get a coat."

"You might. It will be chilly a little bit later."

I nodded, pulled my long black coat off the rack, and held it over my arms.

"Okay, let's go."

He smiled slowly at me. "Hey, I like the sound of that. Instead of me dragging you along."

I laughed, shaking my head. "I just wanted a steak."

"I don't know. Going to this place where the steaks might not be as good as yours could be risky."

"It's Texas. If you can't make a steak, you don't deserve to have it on the menu."

"Amen."

I grinned then, trying to find that spark, that heat. He was nice, made me laugh, treated me well, but didn't have that flame that sent my ovaries to embers as I had with Evan.

And I needed to stop comparing the two.

We talked about the weather, sports, and random movies in the car, both of us not talking about work.

I felt that was more deliberate on his case because he had to know that the Wilders did not like his family.

I wasn't even sure LJ liked his family, but he did come there for work for meetings, and he enjoyed being at the Wilders. Maybe that counted as something.

Or maybe I was trying too hard.

It wasn't lost on me that Maddie wanted me to ask what the hell his father and brother were doing with the Bliss accounts, and I wasn't sure I could bring that up. Not if I wanted a firm delineation between my work life and my private life.

But I hadn't had that disconnect yet, and I wasn't sure I was going to be able to ever.

We were seated quickly, and the waitress grinned.

"Chef Andre is excited that you're here and would

love to be able to work a tasting for the appetizers. What do you think?"

LJ sat back in his chair and smiled at me. "I'm going to like going to dinner with you."

I just shook my head. "That would be lovely, and tell him I'm honored."

"Your waiter will go over the specials and our menu items that Andre thinks you'd like, as well as wine pairings. Welcome, Miss Wilder."

She left then, and LJ studied my face.

"What is it?" I asked, wondering why he was staring.

"You kept your name."

"I did," I said carefully, looking down at the menu.

"Is it weird?" He held up his hand, wincing. "You know what? That's not where I want to start the night."

I set the menu down and looked at him then. "You asked me out while I stood on their property. I work with the family that I was once part of." Though hadn't been in truth. I had been part of Evan's life when he was home, but I hadn't known the Wilder brothers. That had been a disconnect, something that I had tried to make up for somehow later on in my life. But I didn't know the Wilders as a sister-in-law.

Maybe that was one strike against Evan and me.

"Yes, I asked you out while you were working, but I

didn't really think about the fact that it was Wilders' land."

"You can't disconnect the two."

He studied me then and smiled up at the waiter as we were told what the specials were, we ordered our wine, and as a three-course appetizer was set before us, I groaned, knowing Andre was trying to impress, and he didn't have to try very hard. He was a brilliant chef, and my mouth was watering.

"Seriously, even if you never want to date me again, can I at least come out with you as a friend?" LJ asked, right before entrées were served.

I looked at him then, blinking. "What?"

"Kendall. You know you don't feel anything for me, and I understand that. But I like you, as a friend. A woman, or whatever you want me to be. However, don't run away and never see me again. Because I will use you for your food connections." He winked as he said it, and I just stared at him, aghast at his honesty.

"So you don't feel anything for me either?" I asked, then put my hand over my mouth, my eyes wide.

He threw back his head and laughed, and just right there, there was a tiny spark at the way he could laugh so easily. But maybe it was just for friendship.

Because I didn't like LJ the way that I needed to.

And perhaps he didn't feel the same way?

"I think you and I could be friends. But it's nice going out to dinner with a beautiful woman, even if there's no spark."

"Should I feel offended at that?" I asked, then caught a look at the meal in front of us. I nearly groaned at the sight of the perfectly cooked and colorful dishes and rubbed my hands together.

"I know we're having a serious talk, but I need to pay attention to this."

LJ just grinned.

"And that is why we're going to be friends."

I looked up at him then, and he held out his hand.

"Stop. Take a bite, savor it, and then we can talk about the fact that you will never be my one and only."

He winked, and I just shook my head.

With the first taste of the creamy soup, I nearly groaned, letting it settle on my tongue.

"My God," I mumbled after I swallowed.

"Can't talk, having a food orgasm," LJ mumbled.

I nearly choked on my food, but that would have been an insult to the glorious meal. "Okay, I guess we are friends."

"It's not that I don't find you attractive, Kendall. Because I do. I wouldn't have asked you out if I didn't. I like you—a lot. But I also just like spending time with you. So let's not make this more complicated."

I raised a brow and set my fork down, knowing I needed to pay attention to this before devouring my meal.

"I want to be your friend, LJ. You're a great guy."

"But not *the* guy."

If he was going to be so honest, then so was I. "No, I don't think so. Maybe in another time."

"It's okay. I figured if I brought it up first, it doesn't count as a rejection," he teased.

I wasn't sure if he really wanted us to just be friends or if he was putting on a brave face because he didn't feel anything from my general direction. I wasn't sure what I should do, but I knew he was giving me an easy out. And honestly, I was going to take it. Because there was nothing between us. LJ wasn't for me, and we both knew it now.

But at least I was getting a good steak out of the deal.

"*Can* we be friends? Because we have to point out the elephant in the room."

"We're not talking about Evan now, are we?" he whispered.

I froze, stunned that he would even bring up his name, but maybe he should because Evan was between us, even if I didn't want him to be. Even if I did my best not to let him be.

"I was thinking about your family."

"And not yours," he whispered.

"The Wilders are my employers. They aren't my family." I let out a breath. "I may bear their name, but that's for my own reasons, and oddly enough, it has nothing to do with them." And that was the truth. I didn't want anything to do with my own family, so why not pick a new name?

"There's a story there, but I don't think tonight's for it."

I took another bite of my meal before I shook my head.

"Not tonight." *Maybe not ever.* "But your family is making waves and taking strikes against my employers. And I don't know if I can be your friend because it makes me feel like a traitor."

And right then and there, I said it.

LJ sighed and set his own fork down. "I have nothing to do with the business anymore. Not in the way I used to. But they are still my family. I don't know what's going on in my dad's head, let alone my brother's. But I'll do what I can to stop them."

Was this just a good ploy? An act? I wanted to trust him then, but it was hard.

Everything was just so hard.

"I don't know what to believe anymore. Not with what the Dodge resort is doing to the Wilders."

LJ's jaw tightened, and he nodded. "I understand. I still want to be your friend. And I want to enjoy this dinner, and I hate my brother and father. I wish I could just walk away from them, but I can't. Because they are family."

"And yet, you bear their name."

"As you bear yours."

We finished our dinner, doing our best not to talk about anything too important, and I wasn't sure if I would be friends with LJ. I wanted to, but I had been truthful when I had said I felt like a traitor.

And when he took me home, I knew he wasn't going to kiss me goodnight, and I wouldn't have to dodge it.

Instead, I let out a small smile as he pulled into my driveway. And then I paled as I saw who stood on my doorstep.

"Are you going to be okay being alone with him?" LJ asked, his hands tightening on the steering wheel.

Perhaps LJ wasn't as neutral when it came to me as he had said, and right then and there, I didn't want to do anything. I didn't want to worry about that or even know anything about what LJ was feeling about me.

Because I wasn't even sure I could be friends with him, let alone hide from what he might be feeling.

"He won't hurt me. Don't worry. I'm okay."

I didn't say that Evan wouldn't hurt me again.

Because he had hurt me before, never physically, no, he'd always been protective.

Except for my heart.

"Kendall."

I shook my head and grabbed my things. "Goodnight, LJ."

"I'll call you."

"Maybe you shouldn't. Not until your family stops."

His jaw did that tightening thing again, and he nodded before glaring at Evan through the windshield.

I got out of the car and watched LJ slowly drive away, surprised he would even do so.

Maybe he did trust Evan not to hurt me, but he hadn't trusted Evan not to want me.

Only, that wasn't going to happen.

"You can't be at my home. You can't be here."

"I'm sorry."

"Sorry for being here? For making a scene? For ending my date like you did?"

"He didn't even kiss you. Didn't even fight for you." He whispered the words, his gaze in the direction where LJ had driven off.

I wanted to cry right then and there. "Evan. I don't know if it's any of your business."

"It isn't. But I did come here to apologize."

"For what? For being here? For acting the way that

you do every time we're around each other? Or for leaving me in the first place?" I snapped, surprised I'd even said the words. I slammed my mouth shut as his eyes darkened underneath the porch light.

"For everything."

I nearly staggered back. "You know it's too late. You can't be in my life. I love my job, Evan. I am helping this company. And yet I feel like I'm breaking every time I'm near you. You won't tell me anything, Evan. How am I supposed to live like this when you won't talk to me?"

I wasn't shouting the words, I was speaking as calmly as possible, but I felt like I was dying inside.

He looked at me, his jaw tense, his beard coming in since he hadn't bothered to shave.

He had dark circles under his eyes, and he looked exhausted.

And I hated that I still loved him.

"Okay. I'll tell you everything. You deserve that much. You deserved this long before."

Chapter Seven

Evan

The day before, after I fell, I had stared into the mirror at my house, resting my leg and telling myself that something needed to change.

Because I hurt my brother, I hurt Kendall. I just kept hurting everybody.

And I didn't want to be that person. I couldn't be that person anymore.

I also didn't know how to change.

But Kendall? I had left for reasons. For important

ones, but I hadn't ever hated her. So why was I such an asshole to her?

I needed to change something. I needed to do better. So I would.

I had known she was out on the date with LJ tonight. And a small part of me had wanted to come here and see what would happen if she saw me. To stop the date, to tell her that she should come back. But I had to stop being the man that pushed at her. That yelled and acted like I was losing part of myself. Even though I had.

She deserved to know. She deserved everything.

That was why I had left in the beginning. I hadn't even known why I was coming here tonight until I spoke the words directly to her. And there was no coming back from them.

She stared at me, her eyes wide, and shook her head. "Really? You're just going to tell me why you left me all those years ago. Out of nowhere? Why don't I believe you, Evan? Why are you here?"

I put my hands in my pockets and rocked back on my heels. "I don't know why I was here in the beginning, but I'm here. And you want to know everything? I'll tell you."

It was long past time.

"I need a drink," she mumbled before she pushed

past me and unlocked her door, walking inside. She left the door open for me but didn't look back.

I walked in slowly, closing the door and locking it behind me. I looked around the home that I hadn't shared with her. That I hadn't made for her. I had walked away from all of that, the opportunity to build with her.

"Do you want something?" Kendall asked as she poured herself a small glass of wine.

I shook my head. "I'm fine. I'm sorry for being here."

She took a sip, winced then set the glass down. "So you're sorry for being here. Just like you apologized before, just like you apologized for everything. And yet I don't know why. *Why*, Evan? Why did you leave? You never told me. And you would think after eight years I would get over it, but I can't. I have to see you every day and pretend that I'm okay when I'm not. Because you're here. I can't even go out on a date without someone asking how it is working with my ex-husband and all of his family. That's all everybody asks. Then they ask me why the marriage did not work out. Was it because of the military? I don't know. Why would I know any of this when you never *told* me?"

"I'd been friends with Keegan and Ward since basic," I began, looking down at my hands.

When I looked up again, Kendall paled and swallowed hard. "I liked them. I'm so sorry that you lost them."

My throat tightened, and I nodded. "It was always the three of us, which was odd because all of my brothers joined the same service that I did, just at different times. Everett and East joined simultaneously, so they had time together since they're twins. But me? I was in three years after Eli and four years before anyone else."

"The twins were just getting in when we got married," she whispered.

I nodded. "You're right. They were. We were all close growing up. All of my brothers and Eliza. Because we had to be, but there is an age gap. So we all made our own friends, our own families within our squadrons because we had to."

"Keegan and Ward were yours."

I nodded again, my thoughts caught between the past and the present. "We got assigned the same base right after basic training, and that never happens. We saw it as a sign. We were best friends, Kendall."

She licked her lips, her face still pale. "I married you right after Keegan and Lacey said their vows. I know you were best friends. Britney and Ward stood up for both of us, even though they had only been married for two months. It was like a three-way wedding."

She was leaning against the kitchen counter, her whole body stiff as I stood in front of her, but far enough away I couldn't touch her. I was afraid if I did, I would shatter. I just needed to get this out. She deserved the truth after all this time.

"The three of us had a pact." I let out a breath at her look, my entire body radiating with tension. "That if one of us got hurt or if one of us died in the line of duty, we would take care of the other's widow. The fact that we *knew* we could make our wives widows so easily wasn't lost on us, but we couldn't dwell on it and function."

"Oh, Evan," she whispered, and I shook my head.

"Just let me get this out. And then I'll walk away, and I'll stop being the asshole to you."

She didn't say anything, and I took that as a sign.

"I was in the Humvee. When we ran over the IED," I said after a minute, Kendall's eyes widened. "What?" she asked, her voice hollow. "You never said. Nobody ever told me. You were hurt, and I didn't know?" I took a step towards her, trying to do anything to at least calm her, but she held up her hands. "No, continue. I need a minute before I say something I'm once again going to regret."

I nodded tightly. "We were all thrown from the Humvee, but somehow I only ended up with a concussion and a few scrapes and bruises. I was the furthest away from the point of impact."

"Why didn't you tell me? Why didn't *anyone* tell me?"

"Because I was selfish and told them not to. Because I didn't want you to worry about me."

"Britney and Lacey must not have known. Because they would've told me," she said, and she began to cry.

Each tear was like a scar to my flesh, but it wasn't something I could change. I'd earned this.

Kendall did not.

"Things got a little muddled after the attack, so no, nobody told you because they were too busy trying to pick up the bodies of my best friends and piece back together the kid that had been driving." Kendall's face went ashen as I continued. "The kid died first, at least that's what I think. It was all kind of a blur. The impact ripped him apart, and when I hit the ground, a little dizzy, nauseous from the concussion, I looked into the eyes of my two best friends and knew they were dead. Keegan lost an arm, most of his skull, while Ward was impaled by part of the door, the metal sticking out of his chest, and I could see bone, part of his organs. I could see it all. And then there shouting from around us, as others came to protect us, tried to save us. But I was fine. Just a concussion and didn't even need a stitch. I was fine, and both of my best friends were dead."

I uttered the words as quickly as possible, my entire body feeling as if I weren't there and only reciting the pain I'd lived in dreams for so long they were a part of me.

"You never told me you were in the vehicle," Kendall whispered, her voice full of fear, pain, and tears. "I'm so sorry you had to see that. I loved them too, you know. We were a unit. The three of us girls with the three of you guys. The six of us. We worked together trying to figure out how to navigate our roles as military wives and independent women. The girls were becoming mothers, while you and I had wanted to wait. I remember all of that. And I heard the screaming when Lacey found out first, and then Britney. And I just kept remembering waiting for the chaplain and the other man in uniform to show up at my door telling me that you were with them. That the three musketeers had all died together. I kept waiting, and nobody ever came. And I had to be the strong one as Lacey tried to keep the two kids quiet because the two-year-old didn't understand, and the newborn would never know their father. And I held Britney's one-year-old as she broke down in the bathroom, pretending that she was fine for her baby. I remember all of that, all the while waiting for someone to tell me you were dead."

My heart raced, memories assailing me. "I couldn't reach out to you. I tried, but it was hard to get a connection, so I couldn't call you."

"Eli called," she whispered, wiping her tears away. "Your brother called me to tell me you were alive, that you were trying to reach me. And I had to be strong for the others because I couldn't let them see my relief that you were alive and their husbands were dead. I couldn't look happy that you were alive when their worlds were shattered."

I nodded tightly and moved forward, wiping away her tears. I needed to touch her just then, my thumb along her cheek.

She leaned into the touch for a moment before she backed away, sucking in a breath.

"But you did call the next day, and I heard your voice, and I broke down. And somehow, you were the one soothing me, even though your friends were dead. And I never forgave myself for that."

Everything hurt, and I didn't have the words. The problem was I'd never had them to begin with. "Baby. You needed to break down. I get that."

"And then you came back to the country the next week, and I know you went to the girls because they told me. You went to them first. Because of your rule? That you had to go see the widows?"

"Yes. Keegan and Ward would've come to you. Just like my brothers. If I'd made you a widow."

As soon as I said the words, her face drained of all color, and she seemed to have gotten that.

My shame.

"I never would've let you become a widow, Kendall. I couldn't. Don't you see that? I saw the look on Britney and Lacey's faces, and I knew I couldn't do that to you. I knew you had to live your life when you weren't waiting for a phone call or a chaplain at your fucking door. I didn't want you to risk losing me because of my decisions, because of my job. I had already forced you to change schools, to put my work before yours. Was I going to do that for a full twenty? Or was I just going to do that for a couple of enlistments, where I was deployed most of the time, and so we could never see each other? And then I wouldn't get full retirement, and it would've all been for nothing. I couldn't do that to you. I couldn't make you a widow, Kendall," I rasped, my voice cracking.

Kendall gripped my shirt, her knuckles whitening on my chest. "You left me to *save* me? Are you fucking kidding me? Who the hell gave you that right? You left me because you didn't want to make me a widow? But you broke me just the same."

"I had to. I saw them dead, I saw their lives drain from their bodies, and I couldn't do that to you. I loved you so much, Kendall. And I couldn't leave you."

"You left me so you couldn't leave me? It doesn't make sense."

"I lost my best friends, Kendall. I've nearly lost all of my brothers in one attack or another."

"And I lost you!" she cried out, her voice breaking. I wrapped my arms around her, pulling her to my chest as she wept into my shirt, her whole body quaking. I ran my hands down her back, through her hair.

"I'm so sorry. I'm so sorry. That was just what my brain did. What I knew I needed to do. Because I couldn't do to you what I did to Lacey and Britney."

"Why? Why?" She just kept repeating over and over again as I held her close. "Why Evan?" Kendall finally said after a moment, pulling away. "How? How does that make any sense?"

"I couldn't make you a widow." And I just kept repeating that refrain. I knew it might not make sense to others, but it did to me. It was the only thing that made sense to me. And I needed her to understand that. I had broken her because I was already broken. Couldn't she see that?

"You left. Because you didn't want to hurt me, but you did. You hurt me and made me feel like I was less. That I was *nothing*."

"And I will forever be sorry for that." I let out a breath. "I know in retrospect, it was the most idiotic thing I could do. But it was what my mind was doing. It was the only path I could see clearly."

"I don't know what I can say to that, Evan." She looked away after a moment, pulling away as she took another sip of her wine. "I know you still help Lacey and Britney when you're around."

"I try. Do you still talk to them?" I asked

She nodded. "Sometimes. I know it's hard for them to hear my voice because it all brings everything back."

"I know. I promised Keegan and Ward that I would protect them, that I would do what I could for them."

"Just like they told you they would do the same." She turned to me. "You loved me so much you left me. I don't know what to do with that."

I leaned forward and cupped her face. "I'm sorry. I'm sorry for what I did and what's happened in the past eight years. I'm sorry for hurting you over and over again because I didn't want to hurt myself. Or I was telling myself I didn't want to hurt you."

"I didn't fight for you. For *us*." She looked at me then, and I froze. "Why didn't I fight?" she asked after a moment, her voice barely above a whisper. "I could have fought harder, and yet I just let you go. What does that make us?"

I didn't have an answer to that, so I leaned down and took her mouth with mine. "I don't know," I whispered.

"This won't solve anything," she whispered against my lips.

"No, it won't." I continued to kiss her.

"Evan," she moaned against me.

"Kendall."

I leaned forward, kissing her harder, my hands slowly moving around her back, gripping her, and she wrapped her arms around my neck, bringing me down closer.

We didn't speak. There didn't need to be words, not when the two of us had already spoken far more than we had in years.

I leaned back, my teeth biting into her lip as the two of us stared at one another.

"LJ?" I asked, needing to know.

Her eyes widened, and she shook her head. "Just a friend. I can't...that's the problem with us. I can't."

"You can't tonight? Or you can't ever?"

She kept her gaze on my face, and my heart raced. "I don't know. I can't think."

In answer, she kissed me again, so I didn't let myself think.

My hands slid over her dress, just now realizing that she wore a sexy black dress, one that hugged her curves, plumped her breasts up, and made her legs look a mile long.

She dressed for LJ, yet she was with me.

I groaned, my hands sliding up her thighs, under her dress, to cup her ass. She wore lacy underwear, and I held back a growl as she moved back slightly.

"The cute underwear are for the dress. Not for him. They were just for me."

"Okay," I growled before I kissed her harder.

There didn't need to be more words. My hands were up her dress, and hers were up my shirt. She skimmed her nails down my back, and I groaned before I lifted her up on the kitchen counter, needing her taste, needing her.

My hand slid between her legs, over her panties, and I sucked in a breath at the heat of her.

"You're already wet."

"Evan."

"For me or for him?" I needed to know.

"Always you, dumbass. That's the problem."

I laughed roughly against her lips before I slid her panties to the side and teased her entrance. She groaned, her thighs spreading slightly before I gently entered her with one finger to the knuckle. I pressed that spot right inside her, one that made her practically leap off the counter, and I gripped her hip, keeping her steady.

"Kendall."

"Evan."

There wasn't much more we could say. My other hand slid up, over her breast, plucking her nipple through her bra and her dress. All the while, my finger was playing with her, teasing her entrance.

She gripped the edge of the counter, both of us letting out short gasping breaths as we tried to keep up with one another.

I tugged her dress and bra down, baring her breasts to me. And then my lips were on her nipple, sucking and licking, before nipping at the other one, my finger continuing its slow tease. She arched into me, little moans of pleasure escaping her mouth, so I slid another finger deep inside her, both of us groaning.

My thumb pressed along her clit, and she came right there, nearly falling off the counter as I kept her steady, my hand on the back of her neck, my gaze on her.

"Come for me, Kendall. Come for me." *Wife.* I didn't call her that.

I couldn't.

But then her hands were on my belt, and my pants were down to my thighs, and she gripped my cock.

"I need this."

"Damn straight," I snarled, crushing my mouth to hers.

I gripped her hips, spread her thighs, and plunged deep inside of her, her pussy wet and tight around my dick.

"Shit." I froze, my body so tense I knew I would come in an instant. "Condom."

Her mouth parted, her eyes dark. "I have an IUD. And I'm clean."

"Me too. I know you can't trust me with many things, but I want you to. Right now."

"I trust you with everything except for my heart," she whispered, and I nearly broke, but I ignored what she said because I wasn't even sure if she was aware she had said it. And then I was deeper inside her, both of us moving with a frantic pace.

I had one hand on the back of her neck, the other in a bruising grip on her hip, as I fucked her on the kitchen counter, the glass of wine next to her falling into the sink and shattering, but both of us ignored it. She was so tight around me, like a damn vice, and all I could do was stare into her eyes and want more. Want everything.

And then she came, her mouth parting, her cunt

squeezing me tighter, and I followed her, shouting her name before I crushed my mouth to hers one more time, needing her. Always.

And as she drained me, every last bit, I met her gaze and had to hope this wasn't a mistake. That she wouldn't push me away.

I knew if she did, I deserved it.

Chapter Eight

Kendall

My dress was bunched around my waist, one shoulder pushed down, the other barely on, my breasts falling out of my top. My shoes were still on, the heels digging into the back of Evan's thighs. He still wore his gray Henley, his jeans shucked just below his ass. He hadn't toed off his shoes, and we had barely spoken. But he was still deep inside me, balls deep. And I was supposed to act as if nothing had happened. Right? That was what was supposed to happen. As in, I was supposed to just let him walk away so we wouldn't speak about this again, just like we hadn't spoken about the time we had had sex at work, both of us doing our best not to talk to one another.

And yet, I wasn't sure what I was supposed to say.

"It seems you and I like kitchens," I blurted, wondering where on earth that had come from and why I had said it. I blushed all the way down my body, to my achingly hard nipples and down my sides.

Evan squeezed my hips, then leaned down, pressing his forehead to mine.

"It seems we do."

I froze, then looked up at him. "Am I hurting your leg?" I asked, swallowing hard. The way his pants were situated, the prosthesis was fully covered since his amputation was above the knee, but he still had nearly all of his thigh. I didn't want to hurt him by having him stand like this for long.

He looked at me then, still buried deep, and tilted his head. "I'm okay. I can do this movement," he whispered, gently pulling out of me, then pushing back in. Even though he had already come, he was still semi-hard.

My inner walls clenched, and I swallowed hard. "Oh."

"You're not hurting me, Kendall." He swallowed

hard. "We probably should've talked more than what we did, though."

I finally unhooked my hands from the counter, my fingers numb from how hard I had gripped. I reached up and gently stroked the back of my fingers along Evan's cheek. He didn't flinch away, nor did he move closer. He just stared at me with those intense blue eyes as if he wanted to know exactly what I was thinking. The problem was, I wasn't sure what I *was* thinking. What we had done was probably a terrible mistake, considering I had been on a date with another man that night, and yet what was I supposed to say?

I couldn't regret this. If I did, I would hate myself even more. But maybe I should regret it because we were already both so good at messing things up for each other.

"Did I hurt you?" he asked, his voice rough.

I shook my head. "No. Not at all." He'd never hurt me physically, and I knew deep down he never would.

"Good." He leaned down, cupped my face, and kissed me softly. "I don't know what I'm doing, Kendall. I know I'm never going to be able to say I'm sorry enough times to truly make it count, for what I did before, for how I left. I'm not right in the head sometimes when it comes to what I'm thinking, but I'm trying."

As he pulled out, I looked up at him then and let him clean us both.

"Are we not going to talk about what just happened? Like we didn't before?"

He had hurt me with such casual words cruelly spoken before. The way he had walked away as if I had been nothing, but perhaps it had been so he wouldn't have to reveal why he was hurting. I understood now why his brain had done what it had done by walking away all those years ago, but finding that forgiveness was going to be difficult. Then again, like I had told him, I had let him walk away. I hadn't even fought for him. So, was I the one who needed to apologize? Or did we need to find a way to start over?

"I didn't mean to sleep with you," he said after a moment, and I frowned.

"Oh. That's good to hear from a man who just fucked me on my kitchen counter."

He shook his head. "I meant I hadn't meant to do this here, without us talking about exactly what we want from each other."

"I don't know what I want, Evan. Maybe that's the problem."

He cupped my face and kissed me softly as we righted my clothes.

"I could say I'm sorry for years for walking away, for hurting you. I'm going to try to earn your trust back."

My heart ached at his words, and I wanted to believe him. Wanted to see something in him that I once craved and loved and held on to.

But it was hard to take that chance. Hard to even take the chance on myself.

"I'm going to go now to let you think. And frankly, I need to think too."

My heart felt the whip at his words, and my gaze went straight to his.

"Okay."

"But we're going to talk. I promise you."

I wanted to believe those promises. But we had made vows to one another and had walked away for years without a second glance back. Could I believe in those promises now?

I nodded as he set me down, my heels making a scraping noise on the tile. He cupped my cheek and kissed me softly before he walked away, neither one of us truly acknowledging what had just happened or what would happen in the future.

Evan left, *just left*, perhaps because he had so much going on in his mind, but what would happen when I saw him again? Would we continue on as if tonight hadn't happened, or would we continue on as if the past eight years hadn't happened? I wasn't sure I could do either, but I also knew I needed time to think, just like he said.

So, I gathered my things, locked the door behind him, and made my way to my bathroom. I tossed my clothes in the hamper, unsure if I would ever wear that dress again. And then got in the shower, turned the water to blistering, and let my tears mix with the water as it sluiced down my body, reminding me that I was still here. And once again, I was still alone.

The next day I sat in the employee tasting room, Maddie and Alexis talking a mile a minute about the upcoming celebrity wedding. I tried to pay attention, considering this was also my job. I should be excited about a celebrity A-list wedding happening at the Wilder Resorts, considering I was catering.

The couple hadn't wanted a major caterer. Instead, they had wanted to use everything with the resort. Their team had said they wanted to be down to earth and feel like they were at home. I wasn't sure what the scale of this would be, or what they wanted in terms of down to earth, but maybe down to earth for a celebrity was a little different than down to earth for everyone else.

"So, I know we don't have the guest list, but who do you think is going to come?" Maddie asked, practically bouncing in her chair.

I shook my head as she beamed, all of us sipping wine for the tasting, not just for fun, but because this was our job. A pretty damn good job, if you asked me.

I swirled my glass and smiled. "I don't know, but the couple is big in those blockbuster films, so there has to be some superheroes on the way."

"I heard Bethany Cole and Dallas Huntington might be coming," Alexis said into her wine glass.

Maddie let out a little shriek, and I just rolled my eyes.

"It's like you're envisioning a boy band coming to visit you," I teased.

Maddie flipped me off and picked up a slice of brie with pepper jelly on top.

"I'll have you know I did not scream for boy bands in person."

Alexis and I gave each other a look before we both threw our heads back and laughed.

"Is it because you didn't get to make it to TRL? Or to a concert?"

"TRL was before my time, thank you very much," Maddie teased.

I groaned. "Oh, don't remind me that you're so much younger than us."

"Not that much younger, but just on the divide about where we think Carson Daly exists. *TRL* versus the *Today Show* and *The Voice*."

"That's a lovely thought," Alexis groaned. "Somehow, we're the old crones."

This time it was my turn to flip Alexis off. "Excuse me. You are in a happy relationship with Eli. There's only one crone in this room, and it's not you."

"Aw, that's so sweet. Fighting over who's the crone. However, can there be a mid-twenties crone?" Maddie asked as she fluttered her eyelashes.

"Yes," Alexis and I said at the same time, before we all burst out into laughter.

It was good to laugh like this. It felt good.

Like I wasn't losing my damn mind and lost in my own issues. Britney and Lacey came to mind, but after the funerals, when the girls had gone back to their families to raise their children, I had been left alone. We had all split apart, and I hadn't made another friend group. I had tried to once blame it on being in the kitchen for so long, but maybe it was a little more dramatic than that. Maybe it was all about Lacey and Britney. Just like it had been about them when Evan had left me, even in a roundabout way.

"Anyway, this is going to be good for the resort," Alexis put in, tapping her tablet. "Elliot and I are having a blast with this planning."

I looked at Alexis then, tilting my head. "So, Elliot's actually in the wedding planning business now? I thought he refused to do weddings, even though he coordinated so much more for the venue."

"Elliot is helping because I need him, but he's not the only brother around. I'm pretty sure Everett is bouncing around because he's in love with a certain Bethany."

I grinned, thinking about the A-list celebrity who was part of the superhero universe and an Oscar winner. The scuttlebutt was she was on track to get her second one, and if things worked out the way they did, since she was already a Tony Award-winning actress, she might be an EGOT winner before the end of the decade.

"Well, if she shows up with her boyfriend, won't that damage Everett's pride?"

Maddie shook her head. "It's not going to damage your pride if you're crushing on a celebrity. You have this dream-self, who's in a relationship with their dream-self, and then it doesn't count against who you're actually seeing in real life. Because it's all fabricated, and you can still have that giggly crush on someone that you know will never actually notice you."

I did my best not to look at Alexis, because I wasn't sure if we were still talking about Everett and Bethany or the fact that Elijah was dating Joy. Maddie was doing her best to pretend that she did not have feelings for that particular Wilder brother.

"Anyway, the wedding should be a hit," Alexis put in as she went through her line items. "The happy couple will be here to do an on-site visit, as well as their publicists and teams, and while it should be a star-studded event, it won't be the typical Hollywood one with press and crews. They want it as low-key as possible, even with all the celebrities in attendance."

"I'm just surprised that the Dodges didn't get the account versus us. Seems a little sketch that they haven't even tried to sabotage us yet." Maddie grimaced before she knocked on the wooden table in front of us and threw pretend salt over her shoulder. "I just jinxed us, didn't I?" she asked.

Alexis shook her head. "I think the Dodges are too busy trying to take away the Bliss account, since not everybody knows we're handling this event. We're keeping it on the down-low until it does happen, and then hopefully, word of mouth will do amazing there. But seriously, I hate the Dodges." They both winced as I did my best not to look at them, even though I was feeling horrible about keeping secrets.

"Oh, crap. That was insensitive of us. How are you doing? How was the date?" Maddie asked, shaking her head. "I can't believe we haven't even asked yet. You went on a date with LJ last night, and you haven't even brought it up."

I also hadn't mentioned that I had slept with my ex-husband for the second time, and I wasn't going to now. I needed to think about it, and we needed to talk about it. So that meant I would wait until Evan and I had a conversation before I did anything about it.

"Really, how did it go?" Alexis asked.

I looked down at my hands, then up at them. Not sure what to say.

"That bad? Oh, darn." Maddie looked crushed.

I shook my head. "LJ's a great guy. He's not like his brother or his father. Though it is tricky because I told him to his face I felt like a traitor."

"Ouch," Alexis commented.

"Pretty much. However, I don't think it's going to work out. If anything, we could try to be friends, though even then, that feels weird."

"Because you guys went on a date that ended neutrally or the fact that his father and brother are assholes?" Maddie held up her hand. "I'm going to try not to be so aggressive, but I hate them."

"I'm not a huge fan of them either and, frankly, I don't think LJ is either. He's either doing this long con, trying to get into my good graces or even the good graces of the Wilders for that matter, or he isn't like his family. Between that and the lack of real chemistry? We're not going on another date."

"I'm sorry. But at least you got out of the house?" Alexis put in, and I shrugged. It felt weird not telling them about Evan, but I needed time to just think. I would tell them everything once I knew what everything was.

Before we could say anything else though, a familiar voice echoed through the hallway, and Maddie stiffened.

Elijah walked in, his stone-gray suit perfectly tailored to his body, and a woman with honey-brown hair, a bright smile, and a killer dress stood by his side.

"Oh, I didn't know you guys would be in here," Elijah said with a broad smile.

I smiled up at him, trying not to look at Maddie. "Hi, Elijah. We're just talking about weddings and doing a tasting."

"It is a good job where we can do wine tastings on the

premises," Elijah teased as he looked over at his date. "Ladies, this is Joy. Joy, this is Alexis, our wedding planner for the resort, Kendall, our chef for the resort and winery, and Maddie, our tasting room and wine club manager."

Joy waved at us, looking like a bombshell goddess in her dress, and with her kind eyes, it was hard to hate her. Because Maddie was my friend, I would hate her if I needed to, but Maddie was doing her best to look as if she wasn't crushed.

"It is nice to meet you," Alexis said as she stood up, and we all followed.

We all shook hands as Joy introduced herself individually to us. "It's so nice to meet all of you. Elijah speaks so highly of everyone here."

The man in question couldn't keep his eyes off Joy. "I was just showing Joy around before we head out for dinner."

I looked down at my watch and held back a curse. "It's later than I thought. I should get back to work. Inventory tonight."

"Sounds like an evening not to miss," Elijah teased.

I grinned before I looked over at Maddie. "Can I convince you to help me so I can send Sandy home?" I pleaded, fluttering my eyelashes.

Maddie gave me a gracious look that I was pretty

sure that no one else saw. "I'll help for a little bit, but not the whole evening. I have plans, too."

Elijah just nodded as Alexis led Joy and him to the other side of the room to show off some of the wine pairings we had been working on.

Maddie gripped my hand as we said our goodbyes and walked away, and I felt more than heard the sigh of relief as we left their gazes. "Well, that wasn't awkward at all."

"You don't have to help if you don't want to. Sandy wasn't working tonight. I was lying."

"And I love you for that. I need to get over this stupid thing. It's ridiculous, one-sided, and all it's doing is making things awkward for you guys. I'm better now. I promise."

I raised a brow. "Really?"

"Damn straight. I am fine. And I'm going to go make some plans, so I wasn't a complete liar."

I hugged her tight, watched her walk away, and stood alone in the garden, telling myself I needed to get back to work. And not think about the night before, the years before that, or what was coming.

Relationships were complicated. Life was complicated.

And the Wilders even more so.

Chapter Nine

Evan

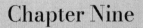

How today had gone from bad to worse, I wasn't sure. Yet here I was, standing in nearly ankle-deep puddles of wine, hands on hips, glaring at the broken taps.

"It's the valve," Jay growled, knee-deep in the muck. While I could kneel and bend and do what I needed to with my prosthesis, Jay had practically ordered me not to dip it in wine, so I let him do the bending while I had done the heavy lifting alongside Amos.

"How the hell did we have such a leaky valve that

nobody fucking noticed?" I snapped and knew that it wasn't Jay's fault.

Jay just looked over his shoulder at me as the rest of the team worked, trying to make sure that nothing else happened. Amos snarled low under his breath as he studied the mess.

Two barrels were lost. All of that wine, years of growing from the vines, and every process of getting the taste that we needed from that blend, as well as aging it in the barrel and going through the entire process of making wine, was lost. While not one of our most expensive, a wine that still was part of our income for the next year, gone.

"I think you're going to want to call the authorities, while Elijah deals with the insurance company."

I stiffened and looked down at him. "You think it was tampering?"

Jay winced. "I don't know. But these weren't leaking the past two days when we checked them. And we have the rest of the staff checking every single fucking piece of equipment in this building to make sure this doesn't happen again. But something of this magnitude? It just doesn't happen overnight. And we're a good team. You and your brother have seen to that."

I grumbled under my breath and pulled out my

phone. "I'm going to call Eli since he's with Elijah right now, and we'll get the brothers on this."

"What about East? Should I get East?" Jay asked, and I nodded, thinking of my other brother, who was in charge of the maintenance of the entire resort. Even though he didn't work with the wine barrels and buildings much because this wasn't his expertise, and is what Jay and Amos did, East was still the best to help fix up anything. He was magic. He would know what to do.

"Don't have anyone clean anything up until the authorities get here. And the insurance adjusters, I guess."

"This will be covered by insurance," Amos grumbled. "Elijah will make sure of it."

I nodded tightly. "We'll get our money back, but it's going to be a hit." It was a hit that the resort could take, but it didn't make it any easier. It also wouldn't go well if Bliss pulled out. Because if we no longer worked with Bliss for their account, that meant that we wouldn't have the buffer to help us through this mess.

"That just reminded me who exactly was at fault for the Bliss mess," Amos growled.

"Same here," I added.

"Don't go over there and make a scene. Punching the guy or drowning him in his own wine isn't going to fix things. You'll both just end up in jail."

I narrowed my eyes at Jay. "How the hell did you read my thoughts when I hadn't even thought them yet?" I asked, now thinking about drowning the Dodges in their own wine. They might not have the winery we did, but they still worked with Fredericksburg's wines. It was a whole complicated process in which the Dodges didn't want us to succeed, so they were trying to hurt us in any way they could, even if it had no direct correlation with them.

Amos headed off to help the rest of the team while I finished dialing my brother.

Eli picked up on the first ring. "Elijah's in my office right now, dealing with the insurance. Everything okay over there?"

I looked down at the red staining my jeans and my boots and rubbed my temples. "No. You're going to want to call the cops."

Eli cursed. "Seriously?"

"Jay thinks something was tampered with, and we're not touching anything. Fuck, Eli."

My older brother, and sometimes boss, let out a string of curses before he finally agreed to it and hung up.

Eli would deal with it because he could act a little more rational, at least sometimes. He and Elijah could handle the front face, same with Everett, who is the CFO for the whole operation.

East and I tended to growl and curse at everybody versus remaining calm and rational. Elliot was busy with Alexis planning that damn celebrity wedding we had coming up.

I froze and turned to Jay as he stood up, wiping his hands on a towel. "Is any of this going to affect that damn wedding?" I asked.

Jay paled before he shook his head. "No. This wasn't even going to be ready till next year. We're fine."

I let out a relieved sigh and quickly shot off a text to Elliot, letting him know that.

"Letting your brother know that all is not lost for him?" Jay asked, teasing.

I rolled my eyes. "Pretty much. We'll get through this. We always do."

"When we first opened the place with your previous owner, we had an issue where the entire stock for that year had a pressure valve issue. Not a leak, but the whole thing didn't settle right. We lost thousands of dollars for that one wine. Not the rest, but for that one kind. And insurance didn't cover it like this is going to for you."

I winced. "You sound pretty sure that insurance is going to cover this one."

"They better. Because if it's sabotage or a faulty valve, either way, that's on the docket. And your brother is shrewd enough to fight."

"And that means I should be shrewd enough to make sure that everything else is on schedule. They'll deal with the cops. We'll deal with the rest of the winery. Because I know Maddie's going to want tours for the rest of the place, and that means we can't fuck things up." My brain was going in a million different directions at once as I tried to figure out the next steps we could take.

"No, we'll keep them out of here, and then you and I will go behind the rest of our staff, checking every single valve they already did. Because I want more than one pair of eyes on that."

"Damn straight. This is why you're my number one guy on this."

Jay winked, though I saw the worry in his gaze. "Good to know. I like having job security."

I shook my head and followed him, making sure Maddie knew exactly where she needed to be so we would keep prying eyes away from this in case the authorities came with blaring lights. I did not want to think about that, but the others would deal with it. My job was the wine, and frankly, Jay and I needed to focus on that right now.

By the time we finished, I'd changed pants and shoes and hoped to hell that Jay's dry cleaner would be able to fix the damage. I didn't have a dry cleaner, and since Jay knew how to get wine out of anything, I let them handle it.

My stomach growled, and I figured I could go to the employee lounge for something to eat, or I could see the person I hadn't spoken to in a day because our paths never crossed.

And I *needed* to speak to her.

I passed by a few guests, nodded casually, but moved quickly through the gardens, past the stone archways where a couple was having a photoshoot of some sort, and made my way to the kitchen. Things were bustling in there, but it was after lunch, and the tour was already going on, so I knew that part of their food was already taken care of. So this meant they had to be getting ready for dinner or one of the other multiple things that I knew Kendall handled.

Kendall, Sandy, and the rest of their team were moving like a well-oiled unit. That asshole had been fired and not allowed back on the property after Kendall and Eli had taken care of him. In retrospect, I probably shouldn't have yelled at him the way I had, or threatened him, but he had hurt Kendall, and I'd seen red. He was lucky she had gotten to him first. I was fortunate the disappointment in Kendall's gaze had pulled me back from doing anything worse.

Nobody noticed me when I walked into the kitchen, but things started to quiet down. People moved about, getting ready for the next phase of their day. Kendall was at the opposite end of the kitchen and didn't see me but moved towards the pantry.

Sandy gave me a look, one arched brow, and I wasn't sure if she knew exactly what had happened between Kendall and me. I didn't think so because nobody had come up to me and punched me in the face or kicked me for daring to sleep with her. For treating her like I had. In fact, since I hadn't told my brothers, and none of the girls had come up to me in any way, I didn't think anybody knew what had happened.

So, were we keeping it a secret? Or were we figuring out what we were together first? If we were anything.

And I hated even going through any of that in my head.

"Sandy," I said with a nod as I moved past her.

"Evan. We're on a small break, so we don't have much time."

I heard the chill in her tone, and while she was doing her best to keep it professional since I was one of her bosses, she also was standing up for Kendall. I liked that she had that because I deserved any vitriol coming my way.

"Got it. I won't be long."

She narrowed her eyes at me, then went back to stirring something in a pot. It looked like a bouillabaisse, but I didn't know since most of my cooking included steak or boxed macaroni and cheese. But I did remember a few things from Kendall from when we lived together.

I made my way into the pantry, the door closing behind me, while Kendall studied the tablet in front of her.

"Hey, I think we're going to need to order more flour. I don't know why we keep using so much, but I think we've been in such a bread phase to go with all that wine. We're going to need to at least add a different percentage."

"Good to know," I said. "You should talk with Everett about that. He's the CFO, after all. He knows what can work budget-wise."

Kendall's shoulders tightened before she turned to me, her eyes wide. "Oh. I thought you were someone else."

"So I gathered."

I moved closer, not knowing if this was the right thing, but knowing it was the one thing I needed to do. I cupped her face gently, leaned forward, and kissed her softly, her lips soft and lush underneath mine. It was a gentle kiss, nothing hard or hot. I didn't push her against the shelving and take her. But I did capture those lips and craved her taste.

She kissed me back, soft and gentle, and the relief flowing through me at that moment was enough to push away every other bad thing that had happened that day.

"You can't do that at work," she whispered.

I nodded. "I know. But I didn't want you to think that I was walking away as I did before. I'm not good with words, Kendall. I never was." I was being as honest as I could, baring as much of myself as possible. I wasn't good at this. But I was going to try for her. For us. Because she deserved this and much more.

"Evan. You're going to have to try harder now. I can't do this. I can't do the back and forth. But I can try. As long as you try too."

"I can. I am. I promise." My jaw tightened because today had just been a long fucking day, and it wasn't even entirely over yet.

Then, she looked up at me, frowning as she studied my face. "What's wrong? Not with us. Well, I guess we'll figure that out because my heart can't take anything else, but what's wrong?"

She was so good at cutting to the heart of it, for understanding that, yes, we needed to figure shit out, but we didn't need to do it all at once. But it was sort of nice having someone to ask what was wrong. After so many years of hiding, because of my own actions, nobody else's.

"There are problems with the valves. The cops were here. We lost two barrels of wine." I went into detail, her eyes darkening as I continued. "The insurance adjuster is on the way, the cleanup being in the process, but we did the majority of it already after photos were taken."

"Someone did it on purpose? They broke the valves?"

"That's what it looks like. The cops will ask people questions, but it's not like they have much to go on. There are thirty sets of fingerprints on everything. And there are cameras in that building, but not right at that angle. So you can't see that valve." Something that was going to be changing soon, and my CFO of a brother was already working on it.

"Okay. Damnit. Somebody ruined that wine on purpose." She paled. "You think it was LJ."

I growled. I couldn't help it at the sound of his name. I just growled. "No." At her relief, I continued. "I think it was his brother. Or his dad. They're the most likely culprits—them or someone they hired. And though I wanted to hate LJ for liking you, he's not an asshole."

I honestly couldn't believe I was saying things like that, but they were the truth, and Kendall deserved the truth after all these years.

She blinked at me. "Oh. That's growth. That is a lot of growth."

I snorted despite our conversation. I couldn't help it. "I guess I'm a new man."

She smiled softly as we stood in the pantry of the kitchen that she worked so hard in. "What are we going to do?" she whispered, and I knew she wasn't talking about the wine or the kitchen.

I needed to be better. Going home alone, hating myself, and hurting Kendall? That wasn't in the cards anymore. I needed to be better.

"I'm going to try to keep this place safe. And then I'm going to try to figure out exactly how you and I work together and *be* together." I cleared my throat. "Will you go with me to this fancy wedding?"

I hadn't even meant to say that. I had no idea where that had come from, but it was a token. A push. It was something different. It wasn't me standing on the sidelines and hating myself and trying to hate her when she had done nothing wrong except fucking exist.

She smiled, her whole face lightening. "Did you just ask me to a wedding that we're both working on?"

I growled. I couldn't help it. "I'm trying to be romantic."

She laughed then, her whole body lighting up, and I couldn't help but join her. She was gorgeous. She always had been, but younger Kendall had been sexy and sweet. This new version? The one who had been through hell and had come out stronger? She was sexy, sweet, and so fucking confident even when she didn't think so. It was hard to breathe in her presence.

"Are we really doing this?"

I swallowed hard, knowing that I needed to be truthful. I needed to take this step. Not doing so would break me farther than I had already been. "We might as well," I answered finally.

She rolled her eyes. "Evan."

I cupped her face, met her gaze. "Let's try. Because not trying is tearing us apart. We might as well try, Kendall, because I can't walk away anymore. And I don't want to leave you behind."

She was so quiet for so long that I was afraid I had done something else wrong. That I had fucked up, but she met my gaze and nodded softly, and in that moment, I leaned forward and kissed her and hoped to hell I wouldn't make another mistake.

Because I didn't think either one of us would survive the fallout if I did.

Chapter Ten

Kendall

My body hummed, my soul singing, and it had nothing to do with the kiss I had shared last night.

In the week since Evan had asked me to the wedding, the two of us somehow deciding to do something with who we were together, I had only seen him at work. We'd stolen a kiss or two in the pantry, but we hadn't gone past that.

There hadn't been any time.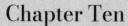

I'd worked endlessly to prepare the catering and the desserts and other items for this colossal event. It was my job to make sure people remembered the food once they left, just like it was Alexis's job to make sure the guests and wedding party had the time of their lives. On top of that, Evan dealt with the winery and clients. We rarely had time to see each other, but I knew this high-octane work would die down soon.

Hence the humming had nothing to do with him. No, it had all to do with the profiteroles I was making for the wedding. I was not a cake decorator, though I could make a wedding cake and other desserts. I was also not a pastry chef. It was in my repertoire, but not my expertise.

Hence why the happy couple who would marry later this afternoon had hired an actual famed cake decorator from out in LA. One that had already knocked me off my feet with her talent.

Because wow.

The cake on the other side of the kitchen was enormous. It could probably feed all three hundred people of this wedding and more, and every ounce of intricate lace on it was handmade by the baker in fondant and spun sugar.

I had never quite seen anything like it, and I was just honored to be in the same room with it.

"I love that you keep staring at the thing," Brenda said from the other side of the room.

I blushed, and it had nothing to do with the heat from the kitchen. "Sorry, can't help it. I have chocolate work over here that I need to focus on, and yet that cake is distracting me."

"I'm damn proud of it. And I'm honored that you're letting me share your kitchen."

I frowned as I worked on the next set, gently dipping each pastry into the chocolate to coat it before I added the whipped cream. "I don't mind sharing my kitchen," I said after a minute and then cringed. "Okay, I would mind if you were messy or tried to push me out of the way, but we're sharing the space. And with that cake? You can have any bench or tool that you want."

"Oh, you do say the sweetest things," Brenda said with a laugh as she went back to work.

Sandy came in, began to pump the music, and we all started to dance just a little bit, the beat making us laugh as we got through the rest of our prep work.

"The ceremony is starting," Alexis said into my headset, and I grinned. She had handed me a little earbud so that way I was hooked into the rest of her team, along with Emily, Alexis's assistant.

Emily was moving around, doing a hundred things simultaneously, just like Alexis was. I was trying to get as much work done as possible to see if I got that dance with Evan.

143

I blushed, knowing that if I did dance with him, everybody would think we had perhaps buried the hatchet.

Only we hadn't. What we had done was communicate with one another which, if we had done that eight years ago, maybe things would've been different. Or perhaps we both needed to grow to be who we were now.

I frowned, going back to whipping up whipped cream from scratch and trying to focus on that rather than the complicated situation with him.

"I hate him," Everett growled as he walked into the kitchen, his hair in disarray.

I turned, whisk in hand. "I can't stop whisking. Why do you hate him?" I asked. "And who is he?"

"Dallas Huntington," Everett snarled, and all of us froze before looking around as if someone were to catch us at any moment. "He's ordering Alexis and Elliot around like he's their boss, and they're his minions. It's not even his damn wedding."

I cringed, knowing the type. "You do realize he's on the premises with his girlfriend. As in, here for the wedding that will all be moving into the next phase soon. Meaning there will be people around at all times. You can't say things like that."

"Now you just sound like Alexis. Can I have one?"

Everett asked as he moved forward, ready to pluck a brie-filled tart off a tray.

"Touch that and die. Your hands aren't clean."

He gave me the oh-so-innocent look that all Wilder brothers seemed to have excelled at. "I washed them."

"Not in front of me, you didn't. Do you want us to get in trouble with the health code?"

"Listen to her. Don't eat in the kitchen."

He looked over at Brenda and sighed. "That cake looks amazing. I might just swoon."

"That's what I like to hear. Big strapping man ready to swoon at the sight of my cake." Brenda blinked. "That sounded dirtier than I meant it," she added to our laughter as Everett blushed. I didn't see Evan's brother turn that beat red often since he was usually pretty quiet, but it was nice to see.

"Okay, why are you having problems?" I asked, turning to Everett as I continued to work.

"The man in question is just a deuce."

"Good to know. Do you have examples?" I asked as I went to work. Everett shook his head and then went to wash his hands so thoroughly I was afraid he was going to peel off his skin.

"Tell me what I can do to help." The man was the CFO of the company but was ready to literally roll up his sleeves to help. It was just one more reason I liked him.

I looked at Sandy, who shrugged and went back over to help the rest of our team.

"You don't need to be back here if you don't want to, Everett. We're good."

"If I go out there, I'm going to scowl at the friend of the groom, and then there'll be an issue."

"Ah. Dallas is here because he knows the groom?" I thought I knew that, but I didn't know celebrity friendships well.

"He's one of the groomsmen. And he's just so smarmy. I know he will be in the next big action movie, and he's 'made it.' But, I don't know. He's just not good enough for Bethany."

I met Sandy's gaze again, both of us trying not to smile.

Everett growled. "Please stop it. I realize that I have a silly little crush on a celebrity actress who I've never met and still have not seen this weekend, but that doesn't mean that I can't think that he's a jerk."

"Why is he a jerk?"

"Because everything he says sounds smarmy, even if he doesn't mean to. If someone's having a conversation with two people, he shows up and adds his own experience, which has to outshine theirs even if it makes no sense and has no connections. And he was sampling our wines and commenting how Napa and France and Italy's wines were to die for, and the little villa that he and Bethany were planning on purchasing was going to outshine anything that he had ever seen."

I frowned as I continued to work. "Well. That's just jerky. You don't complain about the wine at a winery. You wait until you're in your car later, then you grumble about it. How rude." I paused. "Did Evan hear?"

There must have been something in my tone because Everett turned to me and shook his head after studying my face.

"No, he didn't. Thankfully. Because while I can put on a brave face and smile and not act like the jerk, you know Evan." Everett cringed. "Sorry."

"I'm the one that brought him up." And I was the one currently kissing him whenever I had a chance. We needed to tell his family and my friends. Or just deal with it.

Evan's brother sighed, then looked around the kitchen. "Okay. What can I do? Because I need to get my hands busy, or I'm going to make a snide remark at someone I shouldn't, and we'll get in trouble. You know us Wilders, we tend to do that."

"Where are the rest of your brothers?" I asked with a laugh.

"You know, if I wasn't married..." Brenda teased as Sandy joined in with a cackle.

Everett raised both hands, palms out. "Hey, there's only one of us that's married, and I realize that another one is in a serious relationship, but I'm free." He winked as he spoke, but both Brenda and Sandy waved him off.

"Wait, are Elijah and Joy serious?" I asked, frowning.

Everett nodded. "It looks like. Not quite sure what exactly that means. However, they look happy. And she's coming to a Wilder dinner."

I blinked and nearly dropped the tray in my hand. "Are you serious? Come on, follow me. We'll take these over to the other sites, and you can talk to me."

Everett nodded as the kitchen began to empty, the next phase of the wedding ready to begin. "As for Joy and Elijah... Joy is coming to the dinner, which is a big thing. However, Alexis did show up after a very short period of dating Eli. But, they just work. You know?"

"They did. They seemed serious after the first date. Even though I don't think that Eli or Alexis were planning on that."

"I don't know how they did it, but they sure tried. They sure made it work."

And if Evan had any say, I would be next showing up. Or at least after Joy. I wasn't quite sure if I was ready for a Wilder dinner, but maybe that would be the best way of breaking the ice. For us to calmly take our time and rationally realize who we were to each other. Because we *had* gotten married after only two or so days of knowing each other. Of course, things were complicated and twisty. Going slow this time, with stolen kisses in the pantry, was the best bet. But keeping secrets wasn't.

We made our way through the gardens, speaking about Joy and Elijah, and Alexis and Eli, when Everett nearly tripped over his own feet. I reached out and grabbed his tray rather than him. He could fall, but I was not losing any of my appetizers.

"What? What is it?"

I looked over then and nearly rolled my eyes because a certain somebody was the reason that he had tripped over his own feet.

"You should talk to her," I whispered, looking over at the A-list starlet that I knew on sight. Everybody did. However, Everett just stood there slack-jawed.

"I'll make an idiot of myself."

"Well, you're doing a good job," I teased.

He frowned. "Thanks for that."

"Go see what's wrong."

"I can't do that."

I shook my head and kept moving when the

brunette beauty looked up at us, her eyes wide before she put on a smile that was just like every one I had seen in her movies. It reached her eyes, and yet it felt like acting.

"I'm so sorry. Am I not supposed to be here?" Bethany asked, her voice smooth and familiar.

I gently elbowed Everett in the ribs, and he cleared his throat. "Of course, you're welcome here. Can I show you around? Help you?"

"Oh, that's great. I just needed a moment to breathe." She looked at Everett, her eyes widening for a moment. She opened her mouth to speak but closed it as if she thought better.

Everett just stood there before a change seemed to come over him. He rolled his shoulders back, let out a deep breath, and nodded. "Hi, I'm Everett Wilder. Would you like us to leave you alone? Or do you want us to take you to where the wedding is? Things can get a little lost in here with so many twists and turns."

"Oh. Um. You? *You...*" Bethany shook her head, and I had to wonder what was happening, but I couldn't tell. Maybe she was just tired, or I was seeing something that wasn't there. "I just needed to breathe. I guess." She stared at Everett as if she were waiting on something, and yet I couldn't tell.

I nodded. "I get it. And I have to go take this food

in." I took the tray from Everett. "Show Bethany around if she needs a moment to breathe. And then you can tell her where the wedding is. Come on, Wilder." I winked at Bethany. "I'm Kendall, the head chef here. If you need anything to eat, I'm your girl. Everett, though, he can show you around." I kept moving as Everett glared at me over Bethany's head, and I figured that was my one good or evil deed for the day, depending on who asked.

Yes, Bethany was in a serious relationship with that A-list celebrity douchebag, but Everett could have his little crush and hopefully get over it. Just like I was at one point trying to get over a crush that never really happened.

I went back to work, ensuring my team was ready with the food and answering Alexis's questions as she came by.

They were doing a buffet meal for the dinner. That way, people would get up and dance more, and I didn't mind that, though plated meals were more fun for me because I enjoyed making things look perfect. However, we were on the ball with the appetizers out on trays with my waitstaff.

Eli came up to me then, looking dapper in his gray suit that brought out the color of his eyes, and he smiled at me.

"Everything looks great. People are already talking about the food."

"Who would've thought we'd be in the wedding business," I teased.

"Not me. Although I always knew you'd be an amazing chef."

I frowned. "We didn't know each other too well when Evan and I were married, you know."

"I do." He paused. "But what I did know we liked. We all liked you, Kendall."

I warmed, even though awkwardness settled in. "Well, I liked you guys too. But you know the military, they're great about putting us all in different parts of the world, so we rarely got to see each other."

"Well, we're all together now, and you and Evan seemed to be doing okay for the past week or so."

I fiddled with my apron and nodded. "Well. We've all been busy. With this wedding and all."

"Sounds about right."

He smiled at me, then moved off to go talk with Alexis, his gaze hungry. And it had nothing to do with the food.

As the bride and groom started their first dance, I saw Bethany walk in from one angle and Everett at the other side of the tent, and neither one of them looked any different than when I last saw them. I couldn't focus on much more than that, though, because now I had to go and deal with the next phase of the dinner. I went back to the food, ensured everything was at the right temperature, and set to go. People were eating, drinking, having a blast, and when people filled the dance floor, I shook my head and slowly took off my apron, not wanting to stand out with any mess on my clothes.

That's when a familiar touch grazed my elbow, and I turned to see Evan.

"Hi." Why was I so awkward? This was my ex-husband. We knew what each other looked like naked. Intimately. I shouldn't sound like a squeaking mouse whenever he was near.

"What about that dance?"

I blinked up at him. "Evan. I thought you were kidding." Though some part of me had hoped for the opposite.

"Let's dance. You look gorgeous in your gray suit, and I look pretty handsome myself," he said, looking down at his dark charcoal-gray suit. "I had to dress up for this. I'm serving the wine with Elijah after all."

I shook my head. "We shouldn't."

"We shouldn't do a lot of things, but we are. Dance with me."

He held out his hand, and I was aware that Alexis was staring at us, her eyes wide, and the other Wilders were all looking. Even Joy smiled over at us as she stood next to Elijah, though she didn't know the whole history, at least I didn't think so. Sandy scowled behind Evan's back when he wasn't looking.

Well, either the Wilders thought we were going to fight right then and there and push at each other, or I was going to do this. So I slid my hand into his, and we walked out to the dance floor. I did my best to ignore the Wilders and the eyes of people who would want answers.

"You look beautiful."

"I look like I've been working since about four a.m."

"Well, I guess exhaustion and baked goods do well on you."

"Evan," I whispered, my pulse racing.

"You keep saying my name, and it's giving me bad ideas."

My lips lifted despite myself. "We are in public and at work, behave."

"Never."

This was just like the Evan that I had married, the teasing one, but I saw the shadows in his eyes, so maybe it wasn't that same man.

I was just so confused. We needed to talk more, and we were doing better. But things felt like they were going too fast, just like before. And I couldn't let it be like before.

In the corner of my eye, I saw Dallas twirl Bethany around the dance floor, making a spectacle of himself, and everyone just laughed, camera flashes going off a mile a minute. Bethany smiled too, but there was that distance in her eyes, the one that told me she was acting. Or maybe I was just seeing too much into it.

After all, what did I know of a celebrity A-list couple? She was an Oscar winner, a superhero, and he was well on his way in being one, too. They were the perfect Hollywood couple.

And maybe I just wanted to see the damage there because of the damage that had been underneath the surface between me and Evan.

"Where are you?" he whispered.

"I'm here," I said quickly, hopefully not lying.

"Good." And when the song ended, he pulled away after gently brushing his lips against my knuckles, and then he went back to work, and I tried to do the same.

Bethany stood by me then, picking up a small morsel for herself. "Is that another Wilder? He's handsome."

I grinned at her, blushing hard. "He is. And yes, he is."

She laughed, waved, and went back to talk with the bride.

Alexis came over to me and whispered fiercely into my ear. "We are so going to talk."

I cringed but smiled at her as everyone moved around, and I went back to work.

This could be it. If we hadn't broken the way we had before, this is how everything could have been. And maybe I just needed to let it. Maybe I just needed to stop fighting.

Because, for once, maybe I could just let myself be happy.

Chapter Eleven

Evan

I showed up at Kendall's door, wondering if this was a good idea but knowing it was the only one I had. She opened the door before I had a chance to even get my thoughts in order, and I sucked in a deep breath, staring at her, unable to even comprehend what I was seeing. Probably because, like usual, she took my damn breath away.

She wore soft gray pants that floated out from her hips, making it look like a long skirt, and a silk top with a cardigan of some sort, and just looked comfortable. And yet fancy at the same time. I usually saw her in black leggings or black jeans with a tight T-shirt and a chef's apron, and while I loved that, because it was Kendall in her element, I *loved* this too. She looked soft, feminine. *Mine.*

I hadn't even realized I was growling until I looked up at her face, and she raised a brow, her eyes dancing.

"I take it you like the outfit? I didn't want to go too fancy since it's you Wilders, but I also wanted to look nice. Because hi, since you sort of claimed me at the wedding, I'm going with you as your date to a Wilder dinner."

I swallowed hard, leaned forward, and captured her lips with my own. "You claim me right back, Kendall. You know that."

She ran her hand over her hips, shaking her head as a rueful smile played over her lips. "Did I? I feel like I blanked out completely."

I just shook my head and held out my hand. I nearly let out an audible breath when she slid hers into mine. "You said we're going to try this. Because we're figuring out who we are now instead of who we were before. So let's do it. Full in."

"As in full in together. Both of us going to see your family." She swallowed hard and looked down at our joined hands. "I didn't do this when we were married, you know."

When I tugged her out of her doorway and closed the door behind her, making sure it was locked, I kissed her softly on the lips and brushed her hair behind her ear.

"None of us lived near each other. And it wasn't like all of us getting holidays off was possible. I wasn't trying to hide you from them."

"I know. We only had two years together before."

Pain arched through me, and I winced. "I don't know how to say I'm sorry. For hurting you like that. For taking away the years we could've had."

She shook her head, then cupped my face. "I might disagree with how you did it, but I understand it, and we grew into different people, figured out who we needed to be now. And so we're taking it slow and figuring out if those two people that we've become actually work together. And we're doing it. Slowly."

"You are so much more mature than I am," I grumbled.

And she laughed. "Of course I am. But I always was." She rolled her eyes. "Now, let's go to dinner with your brothers where they can glare and try to get all the information out of me that they can about what's going on between us. Even if the two of us are just figuring out what that means right now."

I laughed. "I don't know. That doesn't sound very fun."

"It was your idea to bring me. Now you have to deal with the consequences."

"The consequences of where I get to show off the woman that I'm with to my family. Something I really should've done all those years ago." Guilt ate at me, but Kendall shook her head.

"No, stop feeling guilty right now. We are trying to figure this out. I'm having fun, and I know you are because you tell me, and yet we are exes dating again. There isn't a rulebook for this. And that's something I keep having to tell myself."

"I'm not going to hurt you like that again."

"Okay." She smiled, but I wasn't sure it was the truth.

I wished she would believe me, but I didn't blame her for feeling that way. I wasn't even sure what I was feeling right then.

I traced my finger along her jaw and kissed her lips again. "Let's go back to the Wilders."

She shook her head. "Why did you drive all the way out here just to drive me back?"

"Because I didn't want you to go alone."

It was the most honest thing I could say, and from the way that her eyes melted, I figured it was the right thing. I wasn't good at this romance thing, wasn't good at being a boyfriend, a lover, a husband. But I could be faithful, and I could try. So I would. Continuously. Even if it felt like all I did was make mistake after mistake these days.

Dinner for the Wilders was a weekly event and wasn't always on the same day. Because all of us worked together, it meant that we had to schedule dinner as a family around each other. It couldn't be during a huge event, which meant it usually wasn't on weekends, but it also couldn't be too late because we most likely had work the next day. It was all convoluted, and none of us had the same days off, but we made time as a family.

That's why we had all gotten out of the military at the same time, at least most of us who'd had a choice. I hadn't, as the IED that had taken my leg had also taken my service from me, but my other brothers had gotten out for their own reasons, all within the same year. And when Eli had come up with the idea of taking over this place from another retired military man, we had oddly jumped at the opportunity. There was a similar venue in Austin run by another retired Air Force guy, a friend of Eli's, and so we modeled our place after his. Roy's place was all about the beer and the brewery, and ours was the winery, and we connected the two, using our past to merge with our presents. Which, in essence, was sort of what I was doing with Kendall now.

When we showed up, everybody was already there, and they all turned as one to us as if they had been waiting.

Nobody spoke for an instant, and I shook my head. "It's like you guys are in a horror film, all tilting your head at the exact same angle. I don't know if I like it."

Elliot rolled his eyes and came forward, picking up Kendall by the waist and twirling her around.

"You're looking amazing."

"Oh good, glad to see when I brush my hair I can look quite nice." She smacked a kiss on my youngest brother's cheek, and the way that Elliot blushed, I had to tell myself that I didn't have to be jealous of my baby brother.

"Well, it's nice we can break the ice," Elijah said as he came forward, a stunning woman with honey-brown hair and a sweet smile at his side.

I'd seen her at the wedding, but we hadn't been introduced like the rest of the family.

"I know you've met casually but, Evan, Kendall, this is Joy."

The woman waved. "It's so nice to meet you. And I'm delighted that this is your first time at this kind of

dinner too. So now I don't feel like all eyes are on me."
She winced and shook her head. "I'm sorry."

"Oh, I'm so glad that you're here too. It's a little intimidating here with all these very strapping men," Kendall said, bringing Joy in for a hug.

I knew she was best friends with Maddie, so it had to be awkward for her, but she handled this like a pro. And, hell, Maddie handled it like a pro since she and Elijah had never dated, they worked together, and I was nearly sure that my brother had no idea that Maddie had a crush on him. It was complicated and why people didn't tend to date at work, and yet all my family seemed to do these days was do that. Including me.

"You're here!" Alexis said as she skipped forward, her arms outstretched. I held out my arms, joking, and she just rolled her eyes before bringing Kendall in for a hug.

"I told you we're going to talk. You practically ran away from me at that wedding."

"Alexis," I grumbled, and she waved me off before hugging me tightly.

My future sister-in-law just beamed. "I saw you try to hug me just now. Look at you. Warming, acting all nice and sweet. It's quite nice."

I grumbled. "You're not helping matters," I growled.

"I don't think she wants to help matters," East said

from the other side of the room. He held up a glass of wine, a shiraz from what I could tell from the bottles on the table and the color in the glass.

I shook my head. "Bring a woman here, and you see how it is."

"Yeah, I can totally see myself bringing a woman to a family dinner. Because that's something I would do." East shook his head and then grumbled as he made his way back to the kitchen.

"Well, it seems that we now know who the real growly brother is, and it isn't you. I'm shocked." Kendall's eyes were wide.

I narrowed mine at her. "Behave."

Kendall fluttered her eyelashes at me. "Nope. Not going to."

"You're not helping things." Now my voice had the same growl as East's.

"I don't have to. It's the wonderful thing about being in a relationship with a Wilder. I can treat the guys like they're all my brothers and needle you just like you needle me."

"See, this is what happens when you start bringing women into the dinners. Things get weird," East growled from the other side of the room.

I raised a brow. "Those are fighting words. And you

know our sister—though she's not here since she's up in Colorado—will beat you for that."

"True, but as you said, she's not here." And with that, East grumbled out of the room again, and I snorted.

"I am shocked. Does this truly mean you're not the most snarly of the brothers when you're all together? I mean, it's like my entire worldview is completely shaken to its core." Kendall fluttered her eyelashes.

I leaned forward, my pulse racing. "What did I say about behaving?"

"That I shouldn't even try?" she asked, her eyes bright.

"Well, that's something you don't see every day," Elijah whispered, looking down at Joy standing by his side studying the two of us. "I kind of like this new dynamic."

I growled a bit, then leaned back, Kendall at my side. That was when Eli and Everett walked in, both of them whispering to one another with frowns on their faces. When they looked up, they both blinked their expressions blank, and I wanted to know what was going on, yet I felt they wanted to wait till we were done with dinner before they got into anything.

While I understood that, I also wanted to just figure out what the fuck else was going wrong with this company.

"No more work talk, not for now." Alexis went up to Eli, then to her tiptoes, and kissed him soundly on the mouth. My big ass brother, wide, all muscle, and all growls, melted in front of her.

Did I do that with Kendall? I wasn't sure, and maybe it should worry me, but it didn't.

Instead, Everett came up, hugged Kendall tight, and introduced himself to Joy once again. "Well, I guess we should be on our best behavior. Usually without Eliza here, we can act like the dumbass brothers that we are, but now we have to be good. We have women about."

"I like the sound of that," Joy said with a laugh.

Kendall looked over at the other woman and smiled. "Pretty much. And now though, I'm going to do something very stereotypically woman-like and go see if East needs help in the kitchen."

"You do not have to work," I whispered.

She held up her hands. "I know East likes to cook, but it's in my blood. I'm just going to see if I can do anything. I can't just not do it."

"I can't cook, but I can help serve," Joy said as she followed.

"I'm not going to just stand here alone with all these strapping Wilder brothers, so I'll join too," Alexis said, as the three women walked into the kitchen, and I stood there, shaking my head.

"So, dating?" Everett asked, his brows raised. "I mean, I saw you dance, but you're bringing her to a Wilder event. What does this mean?"

I knew my brothers weren't going to last long in waiting to interrogate me. "I'm not going to get into it."

"Oh, you really need to get into it," Eli whispered. "Seriously. I thought you guys hated each other?"

"You know what they say about hate. It's just one step away from love," Elijah singsonged before he took a sip of his wine.

"Hey, that's exactly what I was going to say," Eli joked. Then he turned to me. "I don't know why you two broke up, and I didn't really know her when you guys were married to begin with, but I like her. A lot. As Kendall. As our chef and as my friend. And when you guys aren't sniping at each other, and pushing at each other's hurts, I like you two for each other. So I'm all for this."

"I'm so glad I have your approval," I said dryly.

"I'm glad you have it too," Elliot said with a wide grin.

Elijah just snorted, as Everett shook his head. "Just don't hurt each other. And not just because she's the best fucking chef we could have. I like her. And I love you. Don't fuck each other up because you're just trying to see what the past could've been."

The room got quiet at that, and I narrowed my eyes. "She's going to come back in any minute now, and I don't want to hear that again."

Eli cleared his throat. "And I'm just telling you that I love you. And she's family too. She's a Wilder. I'm happy for you, but we don't know what happened before. We don't know what's going on now, so we're here if you need us."

And with that, Eli walked into the kitchen. I just sighed, leaning against the wall. "And we're five minutes in, and my big brother's making me feel like I did something wrong."

"How do you think I feel? All of you are my big brothers," Elliot said with a sigh. "And now I'm hungry. Come on, I know there's going to be bad news about work, so let's deal with that while we're eating."

"Yeah, well life sucks, but we're getting better. And half of us brought dates so I'm going to count that as a win."

"I'm not really in the mood to deal with bringing a date to a Wilder function," Elliot said, as Everett just sighed.

Kendall walked in then, a bright smile on her face, and I knew I had to be good about this. I had to be strong. Because I wanted her. Wanted her so bad that I was going to erase all of our past and every struggle that we could have just to have her. And that was wrong, but right then? I didn't want to be right.

We had pulled pork, ribs, macaroni and cheese, two different kinds of salads, Texas ranch beans, and fresh rolls. My mouth watered, and I looked over at East. "Were you in the mood to cook?"

"Half of these are your girl's recipes. Just saying."

I looked over at Kendall, brows raised. "Really?"

She smiled at me, and my heart raced. Damn it. "East has been asking me since I first started here for recipes. So yes, I help out where I can."

I couldn't quite believe it, but then I could because this was Kendall. She always wanted to help. I had been the one to break us before.

It still hurt to even think about being with her now because of the asshole I had been. But I couldn't die in an IED now. I wouldn't make her a widow. Unless I got hit by a bus or a car, or had a stroke or something. But I couldn't think about that, not and feel sane.

"So, are you going to tell us what's up with that look between the two of you?" Elijah asked after a moment, and the room fell silent.

Joy slid her hand over Elijah's and squeezed it, and my brother relaxed slightly.

Eli and Everett gave each other a look and sighed.

"The Dodges are hosting an event on their property and are luring Bliss."

I cursed under my breath. "Are you serious right now?"

"Yes, we are. They want Bliss. They want their money and their clients. And if we're not careful, they're going to get them. Those fuckers over there, that goddamn father-son duo sure do love fucking everything over for us," Everett growled and blushed. "Sorry, ladies."

"I curse more than you guys," Alexis said with a sigh. "And there's nothing we can do?"

"I can talk with LJ," Kendall said quickly, and then froze as everyone stared at her. My hands fisted on my lap, and I let out a deep breath, trying to calm down the rage that came just at his name. "I'm sorry. I mean, LJ and I are sort of friends, and I know he hates his brother and father."

"So he says," East growled.

"I know, I know. It could be a complete ruse, and I haven't talked to LJ since, well, you know..." she said as she looked over at me, and I did my best to keep my face blank, but I had a feeling she knew what I was thinking, and there was nothing that was good about it. "I can try. We can all try. Because at this point, other than going the corporate espionage route or literally burning their place to the ground, I don't know what else to do."

"None of us are lawyers here, but I'm going to pretend I didn't hear any of that," Everett said as he played with his wine glass.

Kendall laughed then. "I'm not going to do anything like that. Promise."

"But I wouldn't put it past some of the Dodges," I growled.

Kendall turned to me sharply at my use of "some."

I let out a breath. "I hate LJ. But that's for personal reasons. He doesn't seem like the asshole that his brother and father are."

"Well, to add more lumps to this lovely cake of ours, the insurance company is trying to fuck us over."

"Are you serious?" I asked, my body shaking. "I thought it was covered."

"It might've been, but another fraud claim has come in, and now we're under scrutiny. So let's not make any jokes about burning things to the ground, shall we?" Elijah asked.

Kendall blushed. "I'm sorry."

"Don't, don't fucking blame her for this. What did we do wrong?" I asked, and Elijah held up his hand.

"We did nothing wrong. But it's the Dodges. Again. They're putting whispers about how we're doing this for the insurance money, even though we would only break even with it and not make anything extra. So here we are, trying to compete with ourselves at this point. It's going to be fixed. Because I will not let this fail, goddamn it."

"We're Wilders. We don't fail. We keep going. And if that means fighting the Dodges at our level instead of theirs, that's what we'll do," I said with a decisive nod.

I looked at Kendall, then at my brothers, and I had to wonder since when had we been in a feud with the Dodges, and how the hell we were going to get out of it.

Chapter Twelve

Kendall

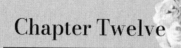

Alexis: *How hard do you think it would be to get a double date between the four of us?*

I rolled my eyes, even though I knew she couldn't see me, and picked up my phone to text back.

Me: *I think it will take a sign of the apocalypse. Perhaps you can convince Eli, but there's no way I could ever persuade Evan.*

Alexis: *I love that you think that my skills in certain areas are so advanced. LOL.*

Me: *I'm not even going to touch that with a ten-foot pole.*

Alexis: *You're the one who started it.*

Me: *And now I'm the one who's ending it.*

Alexis: *You should try. At least ask.*

Me: *I don't know if we're there yet. The Wilder dinner was stressful enough.*

Alexis: *So you're not going to let me live out my fantasy of actually having a friend who can do a double date? For someone who plans weddings, I don't get to do things like that.*

I cringed, feeling a little bad, but it was the truth. Because I wasn't sure if I was ready for something like that with Evan and the rest of the Wilders. We were doing good trying to remember that we were different people than we used to be, but our first courtship had been such a whirlwind we hadn't fully found our footing in who we were as a couple or even individuals. Now we were different people, and that meant I needed to figure out who I was with him because I had spent these past years figuring out who I was alone.

I liked that woman, even if it wasn't always easy to figure out who she was.

Me: *You know that there's another Wilder brother with a date.*

Alexis: *I know. And Joy seems, well, like a joy.*

Me: **Rolling eyes emoji**

Alexis: *I know. I know. I'll stop making that joke because it's ridiculous and stupid. However, why do I feel like I'm being a traitor?*

Me: *I feel the same way. Maybe we should actually talk to Maddie about it.*

Alexis: *But what if we hurt her?*

Me: *I know. But I also don't want to be mean to a woman who has done nothing wrong other than date a guy who is readily available.*

Alexis: *Being an adult with an actual caring heart is hard. I'm not a fan.*

Me: *Samesies.*

Alexis: *Anyway I have to get to work, and I know you are off today finally. So have fun. I'll say hi to Sandy for you.*

I rolled my eyes.

Me: *You're cute thinking that I haven't already said hi to Sandy four times today.*

Alexis: *You need to learn to delegate.*

Me: *Well, hello there, it's as if we're looking in a mirror.*

Alexis: **Middle finger emoji**

I laughed, said goodbye, and set my phone down so I could get ready for my day. Today was all about errands and cleaning my house, but otherwise being as lazy as possible, even though I didn't know how to be lazy. Evan said he might head over after work, but he had a full slate, and frankly, so did I even though I wasn't at work. I piled my hair on top of my head and went to start working on dusting, so I could work on my floors and then go through a few recipes that I wanted to try out. I put on an audiobook and got down to business. I was just about to start working on a vinegar solution for my floors when my doorbell rang. I frowned, wondering who it could be. Everyone that I knew in town these days were working or busy. I had only even texted Evan that morning because he had a huge meeting with Elijah and Bliss today. I hoped they could work things out since they were a huge client, but I didn't think Evan would have time to be here.

I opened the door and blinked, well aware that I was wearing dirty, holey leggings, a crop top off the shoulder tank top, over a white tank top, and with dirty hair.

My father stood there, a pleasant smile on his face, and his wife of two years, Josephine, standing at his side. He wore white khakis, a white, casual button-down shirt tucked in, brown loafers, and a look in his eyes I couldn't quite figure out. His salt-and-pepper hair was brushed back, and the lines at his eyes had increased slightly, but not so much for a man of his age.

His wife, by contrast, was curvy, bright-eyed, and

only a couple of years older than me. I didn't hate her. Because she wasn't a bad person. She never treated me like anything else other than my father's daughter and also didn't try to act like my stepmother. If anything, she seemed to be well aware of how awkward this was, but she just loved my dad.

My selfish, entitled, jerk of a father.

"Dad. I didn't know you were coming by."

He grinned and looked down at me. "I probably should have told you we were coming. Maybe then you could've been dressed."

"Arthur. It's clearly cleanup day." Josephine shook her head and looked over at me. "I'm sorry. I thought he told you we were coming."

"And I told you I wanted it to be a surprise," Arthur snapped, and Josephine just rolled her eyes.

"I love the smell of pine and lemon after I get a good deep clean on the house. It makes me feel like I did a good job."

I knew that my father had a cleaning service but that Josephine also liked to clean as well. Their house was always immaculate, from what I could tell from photos. Not that I ever actually got to go over to their house often.

"Anyway, I'm sorry. Come in," I said after a minute,

walking back. "The house is clean, but I am not. I'm sorry."

"Kendall." Dad walked in, looking around, and I did my best not to cringe. I liked my house, but I knew it wasn't exactly what I had grown up in. Nor was it what he was used to. My family had money, was good at making money, and was good at keeping it. I was not that person. Yes, I could save and scrimp, but I had paid for half of my college and had done my best to keep it that way. And once I had married Evan, something that they had not approved of, they cut me off quite abruptly. In retrospect, I nearly understood. Because I had married someone they didn't know, after only knowing him for a few days. I probably would have wanted to strangle my kid just thinking about it. It had been a stupid, reckless decision, but I had loved him. And he had loved me enough to hurt me—and wasn't that just a lovely thing to think of.

"Can I offer you some refreshments? I have a few appetizers I can pull out because you know me and feeding people, and I have tea, soft drinks, and water."

"We're fine. We have brunch at Dodges later."

I cringed. "Of course you do."

Josephine winced. "I'm sorry. We're here for an event there. But maybe we can stop by the Wilders?"

My dad looked down at his watch. "If we have time.

It would've just been simpler if you worked for the Dodges rather than for these Wilders, but I guess you can't keep away from your last name, can you?"

"Well, the Wilders were hiring, and since I kept the name, it made things a little easier."

"I see," my dad said with a sigh. "Well, I'll make this quick."

Dread pooled in my belly because I knew today wasn't just about him happening to be in San Antonio for an event. Oh, he would've come to San Antonio anyway because his people did tend to go to Dodge's, but he wouldn't have stopped by my house since I was on the opposite side of the city. No, he was here for a reason. But before he could say anything, my doorbell rang again, and I cringed.

"Let me see who that is."

"Oh, I'm well aware who it's going to be," Dad grumbled, and I braced myself.

My mother stood there, all five-foot-ten of her, her perfectly done hair coiffed on the top of her head, and her casual brunch suit looking like a million bucks. It might not be that much, but sometimes I felt like it was just close enough to be true.

"Kendall. You're looking as, well, Wilder as ever." She tittered as she said it, and I sighed and moved back.

"Well, come in. It looks like we're having a party."

"Matthew, will you bring my bag?" she said as she handed over her Birkin bag to the man in his early thirties with dark black hair, pale skin, and piercing green eyes.

I looked up at him then, then up at my mom, and held back a sigh.

"Kendall, this is Matthew, Matthew, this is Kendall."

I noticed she didn't say daughter, but I didn't mention that. I was surprised she would bring him here if my mother wanted to show off her new beau, as she called them, without letting them know she had a thirty-year-old daughter.

"Kendall."

"Nice to meet you. Everyone come on in. I'm in the middle of cleaning since today's my day off, so excuse the mess."

"Oh, I'm sure we will," my mother said with a sigh before she rolled her shoulders back.

"Arthur."

"Gwendolyn."

I looked between my parents, and then between the two people who were closer to my age who were with my parents, and wasn't sure what to say.

"I take it you're also here because you're just stopping by on your way to the Dodges'?"

"I see Arthur has already begun. Well, I will continue since he's taking his time."

"You always did like to go first, Gwendolyn."

I was not going to look into that statement anymore. It was already creeping like acid through my mind.

"You need to help your brother," my mother snapped, and I looked between my parents.

"Excuse me?"

"You heard what I said. You need to help Kenny. He is working on his new business, and you haven't been a help at all. While you've been doing well with your business, you are now connected to the Wilders, who seem to be coming into money. Use that. Use whatever you used to get to Evan Wilder to begin with, and help your brother. It's the least you can do. We're family."

I looked between the four of them, at the embarrassment on Matthew and Josephine's faces, and noticed how they didn't say anything. They didn't defend me, and yet it wasn't their right to do so. They didn't have to say anything about me. They didn't have to defend me. No, my parents were supposed to be the people who did that, and here they were, acting as entitled as ever. This was just like the reason I was in Las Vegas to begin with. Because Kenny wanted to go, and Dad wanted to gamble, and Mom had wanted to go shopping and go to the spa. And I had flown coach in the back of the plane while they had gone first. Because they had said if I couldn't make it when they planned it, I had to go my own way. Regardless of the fact that I had finals and couldn't physically be there with them until the day I had shown up.

That was just who they were. Self-centered, egotistical, and treated me like I wasn't even there. It never made any sense to me, but maybe that was because I had always fought back. I never conformed to the perfect little girl my mother had wanted.

And I had married Evan Wilder. The man she wanted to use now.

"The Wilders are working right now and work hard with their business. And you want me to what, siphon funds from them to help Kenny with some new startup that's going to fail in the next month anyway? No, I'm not interested in another pyramid scheme to help your son. You're the ones with money. Why don't you help him?" I held out my hand. "As you can see, I don't have much, but I've earned what I have. And I told him that when he asked me for money before. I don't know why you're here other than to rub it in my face that I wasn't ever good enough for you, and all I am good for now is to help my big brother, but no. I can't. This is just too much."

"You need to watch what you say to us," Dad barked.

My hands shook, but I raised my chin. "You're in my house. Seriously? I can't help him. I don't have the money."

"Am I interrupting?" a deep familiar voice said, and I wanted to curl into a ball as I shriveled inside.

"Evan, I can handle this." I hoped to hell my voice sounded stronger than I felt.

Both of my parents turned towards Evan while Matthew and Josephine pulled back as if wanting to hide in the shadows. Honestly, I wouldn't be surprised if the two of them ran off together. Even though Josephine seemed to love my father, it would just make a perfect cherry on the sundae that was the soap opera of my parents' love lives.

Evan glowered. "I know you can handle it. You're Kendall fucking Wilder. However, do you have to do it alone?"

"A brute as always," Mom said as she rolled her eyes. "Talk to your brother. You know where we stand."

"Yeah, I think we do," Evan practically snarled as he moved to my side. "You okay?" he asked, ignoring my parents and their significant others completely.

"I'll be fine soon," I said pointedly.

My parents glared at each other before they started

bickering, stomping their way out of the house as they blamed each other for me not living up to their dreams. Josephine and Matthew followed, Josephine giving me a small wave as she cringed, and again, I couldn't hate her. She was trying, but it was really hard to try when it came to my father. More power to her.

When Dad slammed the door behind him, Evan looked at me then and held me close. "Are you okay?"

I wanted to lie, but honestly, I didn't have the energy to do so. "Oh, it's just the family drama. You can't be a Beauregard without being in the drama."

"I still can't believe your name was Beauregard," he whispered against my ear.

I laughed, pushing away from him. "Well, now I'm Wilder, and it provides Mom no lack of puns."

Evan studied my face, pushing my hair behind my ear. "It's true. She does seem to have a knack for it. But I'm used to it. I grew up with the name."

"I've only had it for around ten years or so." It seemed like forever and yet yesterday at the same time. I was a Wilder, even though I was just now figuring out what that meant.

"Can't believe it's been that long." He brushed his fingers along my jaw and I licked my lips. There was just something about Evan. That had always been the problem.

"Honestly, same here. But it is what it is."

Evan leaned back, frowned. "So, I heard part of that. They want money for your brother again?"

"As always. And apparently, I'm supposed to use my wiles to get it from you." I wiggled my brows, even as shame coated me.

Evan cursed under his breath. "I'm sorry. You're welcome to work your wiles, but I don't have much. Everything we have is going into the business. A business that the Dodges are trying to take down, and I'm so glad that your family is helping them do it with their own reputation and funds."

I scowled. "Don't get me started. You missed the part when they said it would be easier if I just worked there so that way I could be with the family business."

Evan snorted. "They just like the cocktails there because they can get drunk before noon."

"They can get drunk before noon at the Wilders if they wanted to."

"True, but I would water it down for them out of spite." He raised a brow, his eyes full of laugher and concern.

I snorted and looked around my house. "I was in the middle of cleaning, and why are you here? Not that I'm not glad to see you, but I am surprised. I thought you were working."

He shrugged as he leaned against the counter. "I had things to do on this side of town after that meeting with Bliss, and so it was either head to the Home Depot closer to the resorts and get done quickly, or come see you before I growl and yell at someone."

I giggled, fully imagining the scene. "Yes, I know getting arrested at Home Depot because you're yelling at the cashier because they messed something up yet again is probably not the best thing."

"I only yelled at them once, and that was when they threatened to arrest me."

"You thief you." I trailed my hands down his chest, feeling lighter just having him here. I honestly never thought that would happen when I was near him. Not with our shared history.

"I had the damn receipt in my hand. Honestly, how could they think I was stealing?"

"Maybe she just wanted to feel you up, to see if you were hiding anything in those pockets of yours."

"Yes, that's all she wanted. My cock."

I laughed. I couldn't help it, and when the first tear fell, I wiped it away angrily, pissed off at myself. Evan pulled me to his chest in a gentle hug.

"Stop it. You don't have to hold me. I'm just annoyed. I shouldn't even be crying at this. I'm just pissed off because I shouldn't be angry. It's not like they've changed anything that they do. This is just one thing on top of another."

"They're assholes. I mean, so am I, but I'm trying to redeem myself here. I don't think they want to."

I shook my head. "You're nothing like my family."

"Well, that's the best compliment you've ever told me."

My heart swelled at that moment and I swallowed hard, annoyed with myself. Because there was always an issue when it came to Evan. I had to be stronger than I was. Because I was falling for him. Again. Like the idiot that I was, I was falling for him. And I needed to hold back. To protect myself. Because if I didn't, then I'd only end up far worse in the end.

"I was going to see if you wanted to get something to eat, but maybe I'll just force you to feed me here, and I'll help you clean."

I looked around and shook my head. "I only had the floors left, but I can get you something to eat."

"You don't have to feed me. I was just kidding."

"I like feeding you. It brings me joy."

And it should worry me how much joy it brought me because I needed to not fall for him again. Not so quickly. We needed to be calm and rational. The fact that we hadn't been before is what had led us to not communicating enough for him to walk away and for me to let him. I needed to be stronger than that.

But it was getting harder and harder to do that.

By the time we finished snacking on the appetizer I had in the fridge, he had helped me clean the floors. I was laughing, both of us singing and dancing to the early 2000s rap music playlist that I had.

"Why is it always the songs of our youth that motivate us to do chores?" Evan asked as an Eminem song faded into the distance.

I was laughing so hard I had to wipe tears from my eyes as we walked into the bedroom, putting away a few things under the bathroom sink.

"I don't know. My older friends usually listen to early nineties music, and sometimes they go for like fifties music if it's what their grandparents or parents listened to. I think it's just what works for you."

"Sometimes I'll start listening to like Guns N' Roses and things from back then, but today I kind of like the rap music. It brings me back to being a kid."

"Well, that's a lovely thing to think of since we're no longer kids, and now we have back pain."

"Yes, and migraines, and adult-onset acne," he teased, and I put my hand to my face.

"You're not supposed to notice things like that," I teased.

"You're beautiful, Kendall. Even if I think that's a pimple on your chin."

He cupped my face instead as I moved my hands down, and I gently punched him in the ribs.

"Be nice."

"I didn't show you how nice I can be." And before I could say anything, he had his hands on my ass, lifting me up.

I let out a startled scream, afraid he wasn't going to be able to carry me like he used to, but then I had my legs wrapped around his waist, my mouth on his, and he was walking me to the bed.

He set me down on the edge of the bed, tugged off my leggings before I could even say anything, and pulled my panties with them.

"Evan. Did we even lock the door?"

"If somebody walks in right now, they can just deal with me."

I blushed, but then I couldn't think of much because he spread my thighs and latched on onto my clit. He lay on his stomach between my legs, making me feel like a queen, yet I couldn't think. I moaned, sliding my hands through his hair as he delved his tongue between my lower lips, licking at my clit, and spreading me.

His beard was rough against my skin, his hands digging hard grooves into my thighs. He was so rough and yet soft at the same time. I knew I could barely keep up, barely breathe. And then I was warming and couldn't control my breath. I pulled up my tank top, freeing my breasts, plucking at my nipples, and then I was coming, his mouth working me to the point of bliss, as I came on his face, whispering his name on my lips. He kept going, though, wringing a second orgasm out of me. I'd never come twice like that back-to-back before, and I couldn't keep up, my whole body shaking.

"Evan."

"How do you want it?"

"I just want you," I said, and he nodded before he flipped me over on my stomach and tugged me to the edge of the bed. He lifted my ass up by my hips, shoved down his jeans, and then plunged deep inside.

He was so fast, so thick that I let out a strangled moan as he stretched me. His cock was hard, pulsating deep inside me, as he stood there, waiting for me to settle down.

"Jesus Christ," he mumbled, and then he was leaning down, gripping my neck in a slight hold, the other hand on my hip, as he plunged deeper. He kept moving, hard and fast, the sounds of our bodies coming together filling the room. He lifted me up, so my back was to his front, and he continued to move, one hand on my breast, the other over my clit, playing between my folds. I couldn't breathe, couldn't think, and then he moved his hand from my breasts to my jaw, moving my mouth to his, capturing my tongue. And when I came, I clamped down on his cock, wringing him out just like he did me. We fell to the bed, me being careful of his leg, but it didn't seem to matter just then. He knew exactly how to move to take care of me, so I could take care of him. I could barely breathe, barely focus. I looked at him over my shoulder as he continued to pulse in and out of me.

And I lay there, knowing I was in deep trouble.

Because, despite me trying to protect my heart, despite me trying to go slow, I had gone and fallen in love with my ex-husband. Again.

Chapter Thirteen

Evan

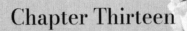

Fire licked at my face, singeing my skin, the smell of melting flesh filling my nostrils. Smoke wafted in the air, and I tried to suck in a deep breath only to choke. Sweet agony slammed into my spine as I tried to breathe, tried to do anything other than feel as if I were losing it all.

It didn't make any sense. Why was this happening? How could this happen?

I looked down at myself, at the blood coating my skin, at my clothes ripped in places, and tried to comprehend what I was looking at.

It wasn't Keegan and Ward. No, they were long gone. They hadn't made it this far. They died with young faces, hope in their eyes for their futures. They hadn't lived long enough to see that hope diminish.

Now there was nothing.

And as I tried to figure out what was hurting, why everything hurt at once and yet was numb at the same time, people were shouting, bullets spraying, and I realized that my leg was too far away. I tried to reach for it. It had to come with me. I couldn't leave without my leg. That didn't make any sense. Just like I couldn't leave without my men, I couldn't just leave my leg behind. So, I gripped my ankle and tried to pull it towards me, wondering why my knee was in the wrong place.

Nothing made any sense.

I tried to open my mouth to speak, but there was nothing, just blood and burned flesh.

"Wilder. I've got you."

A familiar voice spoke to me, and I looked up into kind eyes, kind eyes that looked panicked. Why? I had my leg. We could go home now. I could go home to Kendall. She would need me. But she wasn't there. She wasn't there. Where was Kendall?

"Kendall," I tried to whisper, my voice hoarse, not a scream like I wanted it to be. Blood slid down my cheek, and people were shouting, pulling at me, doing things to my leg.

Why didn't it make any sense?

"We've got you, Wilder. We've got you. Everything's going to be okay." I looked up at the stranger, the man who had lied to me just then because nothing was going to be okay again. It hadn't been before. It wasn't going to be now.

"Evan, Evan. Wake up. You're safe. You're okay. I'm here. Evan, wake up." I rotated my fist out as I tried to stop that voice because they were hovering over me. And they shouldn't be hovering over me. I needed to get to Kendall. Damn it. I needed to get to her.

My eyes opened, my hand out, ready to push away whoever was blocking my way to Kendall, and I saw that long honey hair above me, those wide eyes, and I fell back, my heart shattering.

"Kendall?"

"It's okay. It's okay." She seemed to shake herself out of whatever had made her freeze. No, it wasn't *whatever*. It was me. I had been the one to make her freeze.

"I hurt you," I groaned.

She straddled me, both of us naked from our love-making the night before, and she cupped my face and then ran her hands over my body as if to make sure I was okay. And yet I should be the one checking on her.

"You're okay. I'm here. You didn't hurt me."

"I almost hit you. Pushed you off the bed. I didn't know it was you when I woke up."

"You didn't, though. You didn't hurt me." And then she leaned down and held me and caressed me, and I just lay there, not moving my arms. I couldn't touch her. What kind of man was I?

I had almost hurt her. Had lashed out in a nightmare, but I hadn't lashed out when it happened. I hadn't punched at the medic who had saved my life. They had moved so quickly, even though my leg had been blown completely off, they had done everything in their power to save me, and I was alive because of that man.

Alive because a kid had saved me.

All so I could go back to an empty house, with Eli watching over me, and later East, and the rest of my brothers, because they hadn't wanted me to be alone.

Because I had pushed away the one woman who would've stayed by my side if I had let her. I had walked away because I hadn't wanted to make her a widow. Instead, I had left her fucking alone, just like I had been.

I didn't deserve her. I didn't deserve her tears. So I gently pushed her off and sat up, running my hands through my hair in jerky motions. "I have to go."

"No. You don't get to go. Evan, talk to me. I'm here."

I looked over my shoulder. She sat there, pulling the sheets over her breasts as if to protect herself from me. Because I had been the one to hurt her. To scare her. Who the hell wanted to be with a man that scared her like that?

"I don't have the issues East does," I said, speaking my brother's darkest truths.

Her eyes filled with compassion. We had all seen my brother lash out and go into his darkest places to hide. Because East and his PTSD were harsh enough sometimes that he couldn't even focus and had to spend hours doing the most basic things just to get through his pain. That was East. There were reasons why he had left the military as he had. I had been forced out, and he had left because there had been nothing left for him there.

"I know East goes through horrible things. I don't know if he's talking to someone, but I hope he does."

I shook my head. I had spoken enough of my brother's secrets, even to Kendall. She deserved all of my truths, but my brothers also deserved their privacy. And she understood that. At least, I had to hope she did.

"Sometimes, I just can't sleep. I'm sorry. I should go, let you sleep."

"Evan. Don't go. Talk to me. You need to talk to me.

That's what we promised each other. Right? That we wouldn't keep secrets? That we wouldn't try to not hurt the other by keeping ourselves away. I'm trying to tell you what I feel. Now tell me, talk to me."

I slid on my prosthesis, adjusted it, and achingly sat up after sliding on my sweats.

"I just have nightmares sometimes. I'm fine. I hurt you, Kendall."

"You didn't. You stopped before you would have. And honestly, I was hovering over you. I should've woken you differently. Now I know."

I would've rolled on her, but I didn't have the energy. "So you're going to have to learn how to not get hurt by me? No. We can't do that."

"And you don't get to go away."

"Face this, Kendall."

Her face paled, even under the moonlight, and she nodded tightly. "I'm so sorry you lost them. I know we weren't as close, but I lost them too. And I'm so sorry that they died. I can't even imagine. I feel so...I don't know. I never knew what to say to Lacey or Britney. Because they lost their husbands, and you were supposed to come home to me. I never knew what I was supposed to say to them or their families. Their kids are growing up without their fathers, and while I still write to them, I know that I'm not the one that they needed to hear from."

"I talk to them. Because the guys asked me to take care of their widows." I shook my head. She must have seen something on my face though, because she cupped my cheek, her eyes dark.

"I'm okay, Evan," she said, her voice barely above a whisper.

"I'm not. I didn't want to make you a widow."

"I know. And you're not going to make me one now."

But I had hurt her. Before, and almost again tonight.

I shook my head. "After all these years, after seeing so many others dead, I still see them. I helped put others in fucking body bags, Kendall. Over and over again, I put these nineteen-year-old, eighteen-year-old, twenty-year-old kids in body bags when their faces slid off their skulls, and I had to put them back on so that way they could look like a semblance of who they were to their parents later? I did that. And yet, in my dreams, I see my leg. And I see Keegan and Ward." I shook my head. "I can't do this right now. I can't hurt you again."

"You didn't hurt me. But don't walk away. If you walk away right now, you will."

But I couldn't listen. So I turned on my heel and I

walked away, and I did my best to pretend that I didn't hear the choked sob from Kendall.

But I needed to breathe, needed to feel the air, needed to just breathe. In the morning, once I could think, I would apologize, we could figure out a way to work through this. Because we had to. Yet, was I worth it? Was I worth it to her? I didn't know the answer. I just needed to breathe. And not remember the scent of their flesh burning as the Humvee exploded. I didn't need to remember the sight of my leg next to me, not where it was supposed to be. You know what? I would fix this. Because I had to.

We were at my cabin, on the Wilder grounds, since it was easiest for both of us to head to work the next morning, and that had meant we would have a longer evening together. We could stay up later, though in the end, that didn't really matter, did it?

As soon as I stepped outside, after pulling on a hoodie, I knew I had made a mistake. But I couldn't go back in. As soon as I did, I would see their faces. I would sense their blood. I did my best to scramble down the porch steps and vomited right in my bushes, my body shaking as I remembered their faces.

I remember the keening sound of Lacey trying not to cry and Britney holding her. I remembered Kendall running towards us, trying to comfort, not knowing I was going to leave right then and there.

I remembered all of that, and all I could do was try to hold back from throwing up again.

I wiped my mouth and then walked barefoot down the path, just needing to breathe, to feel the air over my skin.

Nothing made sense, and I still felt like I was dredging through the nightmare. I needed to go back. I needed to fix this.

But how was I supposed to fix this?

I turned the corner and nearly tripped over my brother.

Everett lay in the grass, staring up at the sky, and he turned to me, his eyes filled with sadness.

"Didn't expect you to be up. I expected you to be with Kendall."

"I needed to breathe," I said after a moment, not knowing what else to say. What other words were there? I didn't feel like getting down to the ground and having to get back up again, so I leaned against the tree closest to Everett, not caring to see the sky as he did.

"What are you doing up?"

My younger brother looked at me then and smiled softly, but it was filled with such sadness I wasn't sure what to say.

"I had a headache. And then I couldn't remember something that I needed to. And it pissed me off. And it's too late to call my therapist, and I didn't feel like drinking since it just exacerbates the headache, so I'm breathing. I'll sleep tomorrow if I need to."

Guilt ate at me, and I wanted to reach down and do something, but there wasn't anything for me to do. I had to stand there helplessly as my brother was in pain because of his traumatic brain injury.

I had been thrown around, just like he had. I had lost my leg, and Everett had damaged something inside. He was getting better day by day, physical therapy, his therapist, working his ass off, but sometimes brain chemistry didn't agree.

"What are you really doing out here, Evan?" he asked after a moment.

"I don't know. I had a fucking nightmare. And I blew up at Kendall, and now I don't know how to go back."

Everett looked at me, that gaze still sad.

"You know, sometimes, I don't even feel like me. Like how I'm supposed to be. There's no concept of who I was before. That's never going to happen, but sometimes I don't feel like the Everett everyone expects me to be now."

"I'm sorry."

"There's nothing to be sorry about. We can't go back and fix it. And you more than most understand that. You didn't feel like you for a while, but you know what? Seeing you now, when you and Kendall are actually speaking, are together, and the animosity between you for whatever reason might not be gone completely because things just don't fade away right away, it's as if you're almost making things work. Don't fuck this up, Evan."

I blinked. "What? Why would you...? I can't..." I couldn't finish any of my sentences because he was right. I was already screwing this up.

"I liked Kendall before, the few times that I got to actually meet her when you guys were married. Distance and timing never really worked out that we got to know your wife. And we don't know why you guys divorced before, or why it seems that the two of you hated each other for so long. But now, somehow, you seem to be making it work." There was a pause as Everett rubbed his temple. "Yet, you're out here with me, as I'm feeling sorry for myself. I want her to be our family again. Even more so than before. Because I think we need her as much as she needs us. So, don't screw this up, okay? Alexis has made us better. The Montgomerys with Eliza have made us better. Us together on this resort and winery have made us better. So, figure out how to be you again and how to keep Kendall. Because I want us to work. And I don't want us to lose our family again, okay?"

My throat hurt, and despite knowing I'd regret this later, I somehow managed to get down on the ground, lay next to my brother, shoulder to shoulder, and let out a breath.

"I'm going to try, Everett. I keep trying. I don't know how to not screw this up."

"I don't have answers for you. But I like her, Evan. And I like you. Even more, now that you're not such an asshole."

That made me snort, and then I was laughing, and then I was wiping away tears, as Everett just laid there, his hands folded over his stomach, as he looked into the stars that I wasn't even sure he saw.

And I let the quiet settle over us and had to wonder when a Wilder brother was supposed to heal and look towards the future.

Because, right then and there, it didn't feel like anytime soon.

Chapter Fourteen

Kendall

I wasn't sure if I was more angry or hurt. Everything ached, probably because I hadn't slept the night before.

Once Evan got out of bed, I slowly followed his example, dressing in comfortable clothes, just trying to breathe or collect my thoughts. I had slid on a cardigan and my slippers and had walked out into the moonlight, just trying to remember that I had worth, that I wasn't standing back and watching my life fade.

And that I wasn't the monster here.

But neither was Evan. And that was the problem.

He was hurting so much, and there was nothing I could do for him.

Oh, how I wanted to be the one to fix everything. To make him believe in himself. And yet I didn't get that chance.

I had tiptoed through the grass down the path to where I saw Evan and Everett lay next to one another, speaking in hushed tones I couldn't quite hear as they stared up into the night sky.

They were both hurting. Achingly hurting, and I didn't know if Evan was actually talking to his brother. I hoped to hell he was because he wasn't talking to me.

I needed him to talk to me.

I needed him to know that I loved him. That he could tell me anything. And he had. He had opened up about his dream, about the pain, but he hadn't let me do anything about it.

And yet, was that my right? Was it my right to do anything about his pain?

I didn't think so. I didn't think I had that right because he needed to be the one who did it first. Or maybe he needed to be the one who found his own path first. I wasn't sure.

I knew I couldn't force him to let me help. Nor did I think that I could be the one to fix everything. Because I couldn't. What if this wasn't my place? What if I was supposed to stand back and be there for him when he needed me?

Could I do that?

I didn't think I had a choice. I had to. And I would. And yet, he had walked away. I had asked him not to go, and he had walked away. And that was what hurt more than anything.

That he hadn't stayed.

Again.

I wasn't the one to fix his hurts, to soothe his soul. Fine. But he didn't stay for me. And how was I supposed to trust him?

And that is what hurt, because I needed to be a bigger person.

I rubbed my temples and went back to my paperwork. I had ordering to do, menus to plan. In other words, my job was not behind the stove for now. Sandy could handle the kitchen, for now, doing the prep for the next meal. And our new hire was by her side, and he was wonderful. He was delightful, talented, and listened to us. And he didn't mind the fact that both of his bosses were women.

It was a nice change to the asshat before him.

However, in order for me to trust the rest of my team to get things done, I needed to do my part. Meaning I needed to stop thinking about Evan. And I needed to work.

But I was just so tired. And once again, everything hurt.

"Do I have it in me to make a soufflé?" I whispered, tapping my pencil to my pad of paper.

Maybe not for an event, but for a small weekend. I could do that. I enjoyed making them, even though I was a chef and not a baker, and all I could think about was that French restaurant in Paris that only served soufflés. Appetizer cheese soufflés, a chicken or beef soufflé for dinner, and then the most amazing orange or pistachio with chocolate soufflé for desserts.

My stomach rumbled, I took down notes, knowing I would test them myself, but I thought we could handle it, here in the hills of Texas.

There was a knock at my door and I looked up to see the one man I desperately wanted to see and the one man I didn't want to face.

He stood there, not leaning but tense, his shoulders broad but slightly drooped. It was either exhaustion, fear, or whatever else was going through his head to make those shoulders droop. Because my ex-husband had beautiful shoulders. They were strong, shoulders that anyone could lean on.

Yet he wouldn't lean on mine.

That was a selfish thought. He had Everett to talk to. He had all of his brothers. As long as he did that, I would be okay.

I could be the person that he leaned on for other things and not for everything. I could do that. He couldn't walk away. That was the one thing I couldn't let him do.

"Can I come in?" he asked, his voice rough.

I studied him more, needing a moment to just think. To let my emotions settle so I could breathe and not react. Evan needed me as myself, not as the over-emotional version who couldn't get her thoughts straight.

He had dark circles under his eyes and, though he wore a nice pair of suit pants and a button-down top, he was a little rumpled, as if he had been working most of the day and hadn't really seen any guests or customers.

In his hands, he held a single daisy. A daisy. Like the one he had slid in my hair after a long walk after his first deployment.

We hadn't been married long, only a couple of weeks, when he had been deployed with Ward and Keegan.

Lacey and Britney had caught me up on how to be a military wife, and I had done my best while still in school and changing my career path to being a chef.

It wasn't easy, and I had fought with my parents and been disowned for a while. And in the end, I had learned more about myself in those months than I had in the years after, even when I had been breaking inside after being left behind.

And when Evan had returned home, when we hadn't been steaming up the sheets because that was the one thing we were good at without fighting, he had taken me on a walk, so we could get to know each other in person.

Because letters and phone calls had connected us, and we had written a lot to each other, long and winding notes just to figure out who we were.

Because we were strangers, we might have been married, we might have known so deep that we were right for each other in that moment, but we were still strangers.

Yet those letters and those walks together when he had been home had been everything.

And when we had passed daisies in the field, he plucked one and put it in my hair, and I smiled and fell that much more in love with him. Because that was the romantic side of Evan. The side that told me he was my everything.

"I'm sorry, Kendall. I'm sorry for leaving last night. I knew it was the wrong thing to do as soon as I had done it, and I'm trying. I'm trying to be better. To not internalize everything and walk away when I can't handle what's going on in my head. I'm sorry."

I shook my head, tears threatening, but I let out a breath. "I need you to not walk away when things get hard. Because you did that once, and now when you do it again and again, it just digs into that wound, spreading my flesh and making me feel like I'm going to bleed out."

I rubbed my hand over my chest and let out a breath. Evan stood there and let me speak, and I was grateful. "I know that you're going through things, and I know I can't always be the person that you rely on. But you need to tell me that. Then you need to tell me when you need just a moment of air, to breathe. And I understand that. I know that it's not easy. I know that sometimes you just need to figure out how to stay in that moment. Because I can't watch you walk away, Evan. It hurt me."

He moved forward then, but I sat in my chair, my tiny office feeling far too small with him in it. He set the daisy down on my notepad, covering the recipe of a soufflé, and leaned down to brush his lips against my forehead.

"I know. Everett talked some sense into me, but I already knew, before I had even seen him, that I needed to never do that again. And I won't. I won't do it again, Kendall."

I looked up at him and wanted to believe him. But words meant everything and nothing all at the same time.

"I need to work. But I'll see you later?" I asked, putting out that olive branch.

Relief warred with something else in his gaze, he nodded, kissed me softly on my lips, and walked away, but this time we had both been prepared for it.

I let out a shaky breath and went back to work, wondering why I didn't feel any better than I had before.

"Okay, I wasn't going to say anything, now I'm going to say everything. It's girl time right now, and you're coming with me."

I looked over at Maddie and shook my head. "In the middle of the day?"

She raised a brow. "No. It's the end of our work shift, and today was your admin day, and by the loads and loads of notes everywhere, you've been working hard. So now, I'm going to feed you since you didn't feed yourself, and we're going to talk about what's putting that look on your face."

I looked down at my phone, my eyes widening as I realized what time it was.

Since Evan had left, I had been drawn back into the kitchen to work with Sandy for a bit, and then I had poured myself into my admin work. It had felt good, kind of like I was accomplishing something. I was good at this. I was good at being a boss, when I wasn't trying to handle everything all at once. I trusted Sandy and my team, so I could catch up on everything else.

I had focused, and I had buried my feelings about Evan so I could be that boss.

And I had lost track of the day. And lunch. And dinner.

"Come on, we're going up to Naomi's place."

I frowned at the mention of the innkeeper. "I thought she was on a retreat with her class."

Naomi was the innkeeper for the Wilder Resort and Winery and was currently at an innkeeper's class and retreat, brushing up on new things and ideas in the field. Elliot was taking over for her for the week, and I couldn't help but smile at that thought. He tried hard and was good at it, but it wasn't his thing.

"She said we could use her apartment for this, so that way we have a little privacy and we don't drink in the staff lounge where the guys can come upon us at any time."

I rubbed my temples and nodded. "Okay. Okay."

"Well, that was easy."

"Okay, I can use some girl time. And I'm starving."

"Sandy is making us food, and I invited her, but she wants to go home to the kids, and I truly understand that. She will join us for girls' night one night."

"You're a good person, Maddie."

My friend winked and shook her head. "Sometimes, I don't feel like it. Especially when I just want to scream." She rolled her shoulders back. "I also invited Joy."

That made me blink. "Are you serious?"

"And that question right there is why I did. I'm over Elijah." She nodded tightly, and my eyes widened.

"Really?"

"Really. It was a silly crush, and now I'm over it. I just needed to get it through my system. And it's not his fault that I had feelings for him that were unreciprocated."

"Okay," I said softly, not knowing what to say.

She snorted. "We can talk about it, but not tonight because I don't want to make Joy uncomfortable. But they seem to be getting serious, she went to the Wilder dinner, and I really feel like she needs a friend."

"You're a good person, you know that?" I asked softly.

"Not yet, but I'm going to be. So that means being a good friend. And getting over myself. We're just not going to talk about my feelings, and Alexis understands that too."

"I wouldn't want to make you or her uncomfortable."

"Good. Now, let's go get you ready for food."

I shook my head and gathered my things, grateful I had such good friends. And I did. I might have felt sorry for myself in some instances, but I had good friends. And I needed to remember that and not focus on just the bad things.

By the time we went up to the innkeeper's residence, Alexis and Joy were already there, setting out various wines and food from the kitchens.

My stomach grumbled as I looked at the spinach and cheese cups, cheese plate, vegetable medleys, and Buffalo burgers.

"Oh my. Sandy had fun, and I had no idea."

"You were working your tail off," Alexis said as she came and hugged me tightly. "I'm just glad that you were able to take a little moment away from your long day and get to hang out with us."

"I'm delighted because those burgers look amazing," Joy teased.

I laughed, shook my head. "Sandy is a whiz on the grill, and I bet you these have caramelized onions."

"And this cream cheese spread that we can add to it

now, so that way we can build them ourselves and they don't get soggy," Alexis said as she clapped her hands. "And we set out the wine just like Maddie said, and I'm sure she'll fix it."

"Damn straight I will. And we can do a whole tasting if you want."

"That sounds great to me. I *always* want to learn about wines. Elijah's just so knowledgeable, and I know nothing."

Maddie laughed and sat down. "I will teach you my ways. As long as you tell me what kind you like first."

"All I know is I like it not too sweet but not too dry. But I do like sparkly."

"Sparkly I can do. That's my favorite too," Maddie teased. I met Alexis's gaze over both of their heads and smiled. She smiled back, and I had a feeling that we were all making new friends, finding new ways. This was good. Good for all of us.

"Can I just take all of this home with me?" Joy asked after she swallowed a bite of the burger. "Seriously, I'm in love."

"I told you, Sandy is a genius." I licked my fingers clean of caramelized onion juice. "Whenever we put these on the menu for dinner, they just gobble them right up."

"You say that as if they don't gobble up your recipes

too. You have done wonders for the Wilders," Alexis teased, and I blushed, shaking my head. "I'm trying. Just wait until I have soufflé day."

"I want to marry you." Joy leaned back. "And you, Maddie. This Moscato isn't too sweet, but it's so yummy."

"I've got you. There are other wines that are not Wilder Wines that I can also help you with."

I put my hand to my chest and gasped. "Shocking. You not wanting Wilder Wines."

"I'm not saying I don't want Wilder Wines, I'm saying that the brothers are smart and focus on the grapes that we have, and the ones that we can't grow we do business with other vineyards. That way, we're not making a hundred different kinds that are okay versus the fifteen to twenty that are perfection."

"That's so smart," Joy said. "I know Elijah's worried about an upcoming tasting, but you've got it down, right?" Joy asked.

Maddie nodded. "I do. Oh, I was just nervous because it is a big thing, but we'll be fine."

"Good, and now I can actually talk about the new wine that I can taste the different layers of. Shocking."

Maddie swirled the wine in her glass. "Okay, we're here. Let's talk."

I looked up at Maddie, my brows raised.

"Or not," she countered, blushing.

"I can leave if you want," Joy said. "I truly enjoy being invited to dinner and to talk about the winery things, but if it's too much, I can go."

And that was why Maddie was such a good person because she was getting over her crush and invited a woman who truly fit with us.

"It's okay. I'll talk about it. And you're welcome to hear, Joy. That way, you know a little bit more of what's going on."

"If you're sure."

"I am." I explained about our wedding and subsequent divorce. I didn't tell them why. I didn't explain the utter betrayal and devastation I had felt from being abandoned. That was between Evan and me. They didn't need to know his pain. And then I spoke of last night.

"He left. I'm sorry," Joy whispered.

"Me too. I just don't know what to say. That must hurt," Alexis added.

"It does, and he apologized, and I know that he needs to deal with his own feelings in his way, and I need to stop being so sensitive. But I don't like feeling that he didn't talk to me. And that's on me."

"That's also on him, and you told him that, and that's good. Because being open about your feelings is good," Maddie said, nodding tightly, and my heart warmed.

"I'm trying to figure it out, and we're going to. Darn it. Because I don't know what I'm going to do if we don't."

"I haven't known you guys long, but the way he looks at you? It makes my heart melt," Joy whispered.

I smiled softly. "I hope the way I look at him matches."

"Oh, it does, but the heat? Oh my," Alexis teased as she fanned herself.

I sat back as the conversation moved to Eli, then the other brothers, and then certain celebrities, since we had met a few and it felt as if we knew parts of them.

I laughed, drank wine, ate dessert with the girls, and felt at home. Yes, he had walked away, but he had come back. And he had said he wouldn't do it again. And maybe I needed to trust in that.

Because if I didn't give him trust, how was he supposed to know I would be there if he needed to leave? Or needed to stay.

I was making my own family, making my own connections. And I just hoped to hell that Evan could remain one.

Chapter Fifteen

Evan

"I still do not know why Elijah isn't here."

I looked over at Amos, the big, bearded man scowling into his coffee cup.

Jay was the one who answered, and for that, I was grateful since I was still annoyed that Elijah wasn't here.

"Because Elijah is helping Maddie with the second largest wine club client we have."

"And we are here to try to keep the largest wine club client that we have," I said, speaking of the Bliss family.

Amos was the vineyard manager, while Jay was the winemaker. Together, with Elijah and Maddie, the five of us worked our asses off to keep our side of the Wilder Company in the black. It wasn't always easy, and with the barrel issues, and now this Bliss thing, I wasn't sure we were going to keep it that way. Elijah had faith, but I assumed he was just saying that because he was looking at it through the eyes of his relationship with Joy.

"Let's get to it," Jay said as he looked over my shoulder, and I turned to see two of the Bliss sons walking towards us.

We had chosen a local café for coffee and brunch. It wasn't a fancy place. It wasn't a place on any top-ten maps of our local area. But it was one of our favorite places to go, and it was quiet. This way, we weren't meeting on Wilder grounds. Maybe we could just see what was going on with this family in a more casual setting.

Antonio and Michael Bliss walked towards us, and I stood up, gesturing towards our table in the corner.

Both men looked tired, and I wasn't sure that was a good way to start, but I had to hope this led to something. I wasn't sure what Wilder Wines would do if we lost Bliss. That, on top of the other problems we had, was an issue.

"Antonio, Michael, thanks for meeting us."

"I love their club sandwiches, so I'm glad I'm here,"

Michael said with a grin, and Antonio just rolled his eyes.

"We're sorry, it's just the two of us. David's at home with the newborn with his wife. It's colic."

"Give him our best," I said, wincing at the thought. *Poor kid.*

"Colic's the thing that causes a lot of coughing, right?" Amos asked, and Michael nodded.

"It's not fun. We love our nephew, but all he does is scream right now. I know it's not easy for his mom and dad, nor is it easy for him."

"Well, I'm sorry that he has to deal with that. I hope that colic goes away quickly," I said, gesturing towards the table. "Do you want to take a seat?"

"That sounds great," Antonio said as he looked at me. "And I noticed you didn't even ask why our dad wasn't here."

I met the other man's gaze. "I assumed he wasn't going to show up. The offer was for the entire Bliss family."

"Well, if either of us were married, we would've brought our wives, but sadly, we're the single ones."

Antonio pinched the bridge of his nose. "Well, thanks for that," the older Bliss brother said with a sigh. "And yes, Dad knows we're here, but he is being an asshole right now."

Michael's shoulders dropped as he sat down at the table and looked over the menu. "He always has been, Antonio. It's why he keeps saying he wants to retire and hasn't yet."

I leaned forward, perking up. "He wants to leave?"

Antonio scowled at Michael, and I wasn't sure he was supposed to say anything.

"Yes. Jefferson Bliss wants to retire, or wants to make sure we know what we're doing first," he added dryly.

"Meaning he's trying to do things his way and not listening to you?" Jay asked as Amos sat back silently, like usual, studying everyone.

"We don't want to lose Wilder Wines, just like we didn't want to lose the company before you."

I blinked, surprised at Antonio's candor. The other man must have seen it on my face because he smirked.

"My dad's in a pissing contest with you because he's friends with Dodge. But you already knew that?" he asked, and I nodded, figuring if they were going to put their cards on the table, so would I.

"Dodge doesn't like this because he thinks we're competition. Even though we cater to two different clienteles, and we could have worked together like we do with the place up in Austin."

"Roy's place. I wished we worked with beer as much

as we did wine because his brewery is fantastic," Michael put in.

"Exactly. Dodge doesn't like us; he thinks we're outsiders."

"And my dad thinks the same. Until we have full reign, I don't know what we can do because we're not a majority. Dad holds the majority."

My hopes fell, but I tried not to let it show on my face, and I gestured towards the menu. "Well, then let's eat. Because other than waiting for your dad to retire, I am not sure what we can do right now."

"We're here because we're on your side, and we'll do what we can, but our company's a family company, and you know how that is," Antonio said after a moment.

I nodded, knowing what he meant and hoping to hell there was a way to fix it.

Brunch went surprisingly well, as we got to know the two of the three Bliss brothers, and I found that I liked them. I figured my brothers would, too. We needed more connections in this area.

Antonio and Michael left first, with Amos following, wanting to check on his grapes. Which left me with the bill, but I just sighed, knowing Elijah would take care of it.

"That went better than expected," Jay said as he folded his hands over his stomach.

I blinked over at my friend. "Really?"

"Seriously. They could not have shown up, or shown up and twirled their mustaches like villains. Instead, they explained that their father is the evil mustache twirler."

"Well, that makes sense. It seems like the older generation doesn't like us."

Jay's face paled, and then his jaw tightened. "Look who's here; seems like you can't go anywhere these days."

I turned to see Brayden moving closer, grinning in our direction.

"Well then, look who I see here. Meeting with Bliss? Too bad they're working with us now. You should just give up. There's no way you can be in this business. You're nothing but a bunch of roughnecks."

"I thought roughnecks worked with oil?" Jay asked. "I work with wine."

I didn't want to make a scene, so I just shook my head. "Is there something that you want, Brayden?"

"I want you to leave, but that's not going to happen, so I want your place to fail. How's that?"

I wanted to ask him why he had broken our taps, why he had tried to take so much from us. How he had gotten onto our land and hurt our business, but I couldn't. Because the cops were still trying to figure it out, and the insurance company was still waiting on that report. Meaning I could do nothing. And even though rage simmered inside me, I stopped. Because if I fucked this up for my family, I would never forgive myself.

"If you're done, we're heading out. Some people have to work."

"Don't worry. I promise you'll get what you want. Or at least I will." Brayden turned on his heel and left, and I just stared after him, confused.

"Now he's the one that needs to be twirling a mustache," Jay put in, and I sighed, standing up, ignoring the pain in my leg. I'd had a long day. Whenever I was stressed, that phantom pain came back with a vengeance.

"I don't know what he wants. But I don't think he was here to spy on us."

"No, I don't think so either. He came over from a table with a woman. He was here for a lunch date. In the middle of a workday."

"I don't care how or when he works, as long as he doesn't hurt our business. What I told Antonio and Michael was true. If we could work with them, I would."

Jay's eyes widened. "Seriously? After all they've done?"

"If they did it, then I want consequences. But if they didn't? Fuck yeah, I'd work with them. I want to make things easier for us. I'm just so tired of everything being exhausting."

We made our way out, and I got in the passenger seat of Jay's truck.

"I want things easier for your family, too, and for mine. But, I don't know, something just feels off, you know?"

That dread settled in my gut, and I nodded tightly. "I don't know what Brayden meant by that. Is he going to hit the winery again? Or another client?"

"And call your brothers, let them know what happened, just in case."

"We have cameras in place, but let's double-check," I said as I pulled out my phone and began to text my brothers, hoping to hell that we weren't going to have to deal with the Dodge family any time soon.

Later, with nothing else for me to do after a long day, I headed back towards the kitchen, hoping that at least I could do this right.

I was hungry, a little growly, but I wanted to see one person.

Kendall looked up from the stove and smiled up at me.

"Hi there. Are you ready to go?"

"I am."

"Are you up for a date tonight?" She moved away from the stove and wiped her hands on her apron.

"I am if you are. I want to be with you outside of the Wilder area. You know?"

She smiled up at me, her gaze searching. "Let me go tell Alexander I'm ready to go, and then I will get my things."

"Sorry we're not going to someplace fancy, but I figured my little barbecue joint is good enough for us, right?"

"As long as I don't have to shower again and do up my hair and makeup completely, I'm really happy."

I smiled and realized that we were acting like an old married couple once again, but I liked it. I just had to hope that we weren't following the same steps we had before. Or maybe I was just worried that I was the one that was going to follow in the same steps.

Kendall gathered her things, and we made our way to the barbecue place that had butcher paper on trays in place of plates, and everything smelled of brisket, barbecue sauce, and good smoke.

Kendall groaned as she took a bite of her chicken and then did a little chair dance.

"Good?" I asked, falling that much more in love with her at her happiness over smoked chicken.

"It is so juicy and good. And I know there's a dirty joke there, but just let me have this."

"We got enough meat for a family of four, so have whatever you want."

"Oh, I think we could get through this plus the green beans, the Texas beans, plus the bread, onions, and pickles? This is the best Texas barbecue ever."

"Which sauces are you using?"

"I mix the Inferno and the Sweet and Spicy."

"I did the Diablo, but now I kind of want yours."

"You can have anything you want. I'm easy." She winked, and I shook my head.

"Don't say that when we're just going home together."

She rolled her eyes. "This is nice. I know you had a hard afternoon, and I've been cooking all day, but this is nice. We don't do this."

I looked around at the couples and families all around us and shrugged. "We didn't do this before, did we?"

"We didn't. We did things a little backward, and we didn't have a lot of money. But I cooked for you at home, and I tried out new recipes, and we went out with the guys." She cringed. "I'm sorry."

I shook my head, leaned forward, and took her hand. "No, we should talk about Ward and Keegan, Lacey and

Britney. Because I didn't for so long, and that's partially why I acted as I did."

"The six of us were a crew. And I hate that they're gone, and I hate that I've lost touch with the girls. But we had our own lives for those two years."

"And we made it work until I didn't."

"Again, I let you walk away, I didn't fight. And that's on me, too. But I don't want to talk about that. We're getting to know who we are now. And we are completely different people. We could have grown together, but we grew as who we are now, and we're figuring it out."

"And I keep fucking up here. As the man I am now."

"Am I worried about the fact that we could make the same mistakes? Yes. Because we're falling into this just as quickly as we did before."

Our food lay untouched between us and I leaned forward, brushing her hair away from her face.

"Serious talk for a casual dinner."

"You're right. And I need to stop thinking about what could happen and trust in what we have."

"You're taking the words right out of my mouth."

"Well then, let's put some brisket inside both of our mouths, and not worry about what we can't control, and try to fix what we can."

"Deal."

And then I broke off a piece of brisket, handed it to her, and she ate it right out of my hands, rolling her eyes.

"Sexy," she mumbled, and I laughed, knowing that we weren't out of the woods yet. We had a long way to go. Because she didn't trust me yet. I knew that. I had a feeling that she didn't like the fact that she didn't trust me. I had broken that trust by walking away more than once, and now I needed to fix it.

I also realized that I wasn't the only one thinking we were falling too fast again.

But with Kendall, had I ever really fallen out of love with her? Perhaps that was a problem.

We made our way back to my place, and as soon as the door closed, she jumped on me.

I laughed, caught her, and pinned her against the door.

"Really?"

"I can't help it. Barbecue does things to me."

I laughed, my face pressed against her neck.

"Looks like I'm going to have to buy a smoker for this place."

"Oh yes. That's going to do it for me. Those wood chips? Oh yeah, do me, baby."

My shoulders shook as I laughed, her body sliding down me. And then she moved quickly, pinning me to the doorway.

"What are you doing?"

"What I've been thinking about when we were eating barbecue, and that sausage looked so yummy."

"Please do not bite my dick. And let's not describe my penis in any way with 'sausage' or 'bratwurst.' There are lines."

"As soon as I said it, I knew it was wrong, but I still want your dick in my mouth."

"I love when you talk that way."

"I can't believe I just said that out loud, so let me go."

She giggled and then undid my pants.

Before I could help her, I was groaning, my eyes crossing as she swallowed me whole, the tip of my cock pressing against the back of her throat. She hummed, and then somehow I went deeper, my whole body shaking. She had one hand on the base of my dick, the other cupping my balls after she wiggled my pants down below my ass. And then I was moving, unable to stop myself, as I fucked her mouth, warm and hot and slick.

She worked me as if she knew every inch of me, and I kept moving, not wanting to go too fast but unable to stop. Because it was all I could do not to go harder and come right down her throat. When I was close, my balls tightening, I moved away, shaking my head. I squeezed the base of my dick, willing myself not to come.

"I want in that pussy. I don't want to come right now."

"Spoilsport." And then she stood up quickly, stripped off her shirt, and ran towards the bedroom.

Her bra came next, and then a shoe, then the other. And then her pants were flowing behind her as I followed her, going slower, stalking. Because she would be right where I wanted her as soon as I got to the bedroom. I knew it.

She lay in the middle of the bed, her legs spread, one hand on her nipple, the other between her delicate folds as she played with herself, her fingers playing over her clit, spreading herself for me.

She was pink and wet and luscious, and I dove for her, needing my mouth on her cunt. She nearly shot off the bed as I leaned down, then licked and sucked, spreading her pussy for me so I could tongue her with my mouth.

"Evan."

She moaned again, and I kept going, needing her. I speared her with one finger, then two, then stretched her with a third, as she shook, both hands on her breasts as she neared her orgasm. And when I blew on her and then twisted my lips over her clit, she came on my face, her body shaking, her pussy drenching me.

"Evan. I need you."

I nodded tightly and then stripped off my clothes before I heaved myself on the bed and laid down on my back.

"The leg's hurting me, babe. Do you mind doing the work?"

She slid her hands through her mane of hair and laughed. "I think I can."

She hovered over me, and I gripped the base of my dick, and then she was sinking down onto me, her wet heat squeezing me like a vice.

She looked like a goddess, her breasts full and tight, her hips flaring out. I slid both of my hands up her thighs to her hips, keeping her steady as she rocked, rubbing her clit along the base of my cock.

"Are you going to come like that, baby?" I growled.

"Make me come, Evan. Please, and then I'll ride you."

"As my lady wishes." I sat up slightly, so I could suck one nipple into my mouth. She gasped, and then I played with her clit, my thumb pressing her hard, and when she rocked against me, grinding, she finally came, her pussy tightening around me so much I nearly followed her. But I held strong, holding back, doing my best to make this the most pleasurable experience for her.

And when she moved, she looked like a cat in cream

and put both hands on my shoulders before she slid up my cock and slammed back down again.

We both groaned, and then she moved, both of us shifting with wild abandon.

I couldn't breathe, couldn't focus. It was all Kendall. Just her.

There were no worries, no pasts, no futures, no truths, no lies.

Just Kendall.

And when I came, she followed me, her whole body pink and sweaty, and then she was laying on top of me, breaths coming out in harsh pants, and I tried to speak, tried to do anything. But there was nothing.

So I slid one hand over her ass, the other on the back of her neck, and just held her close.

I couldn't let her go. Couldn't let this end.

And that meant I would have to do anything to keep it. I'd have to do anything to keep her.

Chapter Sixteen

Kendall

Evan: *Stay as long as you need. You worked late last night. I like you in my bed when I wake up in the morning.*

I grinned, though he couldn't see me, and my heart warmed.

The night before, I had worked until far too late after the rest of the kitchen had closed, going through inventory and upcoming recipes. We had a large event in two days and a wedding the day after. I knew Elliot and Alexis didn't like booking such big events back-to-back since it put a strain on all of us, but this scheduling thing had to happen. And that meant today I had a full day at home. I wouldn't call it a day off because I planned to still work in Evan's kitchen to get a few recipes fine-tuned and to make sure that I had everything ready, but I could take a long morning to soak in the tub and to plan my meal for the evening. Because tonight I was cooking for Evan. Just the two of us, a romantic meal. Although some people might not think that would be fun since it was also my job, it was exactly what I wanted.

I loved being able to cook for him. It felt like I was giving him part of myself. It was absolute perfection when Evan groaned in just the right ways when he tasted my food.

Me: *You woke me up when you got out of bed but in the best way possible.*

I blushed and continued texting.

Me: *And then I took a long hot bath, and though you didn't have bubbles, the warm water was perfect for my sore nipples after last night.*

I blushed even harder. I couldn't believe I was texting these words to Evan. It didn't matter that I could say it to him in person. Texting felt like something different.

Evan: *Woman. I'm at work. And now with a hard-on. And I have to go meet with Elijah and an inspector* from the insurance company. With my dick pressing against my zipper. Thank you.

Evan: *Keep doing it.*

I laughed out loud and set my phone down, shaking my head. I wasn't sure where we stood, the two of us, but we were getting better—figuring out our path. I had to put all that aside, work on my schedule, and get ready.

I was enjoying myself, even though it was odd to think that I was with Evan again after so many years of being angry and hating part of myself and him, and yet we were making this work. Damn it. He was adhering to his promises, and I was trusting that. I was happy.

That should scare me, and it didn't.

My phone buzzed again, and I bit my lip, wondering what Evan was going to say now.

Only it wasn't Evan.

"Hey there. I wasn't expecting a call."

LJ and I were friends. Somewhat. We were getting there. And Evan wasn't even all that jealous. Yes, he got grumbly, but things were going so well between the two of us that LJ was just on the periphery. He was a man that I had gone out to dinner with as a friend. Nothing more.

It wasn't like LJ and I even saw each other, considering we only talked on the phone or met in passing in the dining room at the resort.

"Hey. I know it's weird for me to call you out of the blue since I usually only see you when I'm starving and with clients at your place, but I wanted to update you on a few things."

I tensed. "Do I want to know?"

LJ cleared his throat. "No. You don't. My dad and brother are assholes."

That made me burst out laughing, and I shook my head even though he couldn't see me. "I don't know if that is exactly new information. Sorry."

LJ's laugh was deep through the phone. "Oh, don't be sorry. I'm the one who's sorry. They're assholes. And they have completely shut me out on this Bliss thing."

My hopes plummeted and I leaned against the fridge, shaking my head. "Damn it. I know you're trying, and I know that your father and brother are the jerks in this, but I don't understand it. It's not like they have a wine club. Do they just want to take away any money that the Bliss people can bring in?"

"That's what it's looking like. Old man Bliss and my dad are friends, and Bliss will find another winery, with Dodge being the middleman. In the end, it's going to cost everyone more money, so I don't understand what the fuck is going on." He paused. "Sorry for my language."

I burst out laughing. "LJ. I'm a Wilder. I curse more than you."

There was a pause, and I was afraid I had said something wrong. "LJ?" I whispered.

"No. You sound happier. I like it. And yes, you are a Wilder. And you always have been. I'm glad that we're friends, Kendall. That things aren't weird between the two of us."

"Oh, things are weird, but we're making do."

"Look at you with the truth. Just throwing it out there like that. You're right. Things are weird. And maybe one day, when I actually find someone serious to date in the whole eight minutes of time I have a day, we can go on a double date. I'm sure Evan won't want to throttle me if I bring someone."

"We'll see if Evan ever thinks that's a good idea."

"We both know that Evan will punch me the first time he sees me."

"He won't, because he knows I'm not a huge fan of violence. And because he knows we're just friends."

"We'll see. But I wouldn't blame him. I mean, I did take his wife out for dinner. On a date."

"Whatever. Thanks for trying with Bliss, though," I said, changing the subject.

It was odd that I didn't correct him on the whole wife thing. Because I was Evan's ex-wife, but now I was his girlfriend? We hadn't actually put any labels on what we were. Just that we were each other's, and that should be enough. Shouldn't it?

Before I let myself go down that scary line of thought, I forced myself to get back into the conversation.

"I'm heading over to Wilder's now," he said, surprising me.

"Really?" Now *that* was a surprise.

"I'm going to talk with Eli. To see what I can do. Because maybe working with Eli will be a deterrent. I don't know. I have my own clients, my own job, and if I work with Wilder, rather than just doing my work at your restaurant when I'm there, maybe it'll change my dad's mind."

"LJ. That's a big step."

"I'm just fucking tired of my family trying to destroy your family's company because they want to. And if the Dodges aren't going to let me do my job, then I'll do it for the Wilders. And we'll all succeed."

My lips twitched, and I grinned. "Your dad's not going to know what hit him."

"He's going to disown me, but it's fine. He shouldn't have let me do so much of the contracts for as long as I did. Because he can't hurt me."

I wanted to hope that was true, but I wasn't sure.

"I'll be in the kitchen later. You can come back for lunch if you want. Maybe talk to Evan."

"Maybe. Let's see how this meeting with Eli goes."

We said our goodbyes, and I hung up and got back to work. I wasn't working today in the kitchen, but I wanted to go through a few things from home. At Evan's home. Somewhere that almost felt like mine, though we alternated whose house we spent the night at. While it was easier to be here for work, I also didn't want to live and work at the same place. I lit the stove and set water to boil to work on a recipe before I headed over for lunch. It was still early enough in the day—since Evan woke before the sun rose—that I had time to do one recipe and then head to my industrial kitchen.

I turned on music and shook my hips to Shakira as I went through my list of things I needed.

I was just picking out the pasta as the water continued to heat when the lights went out in the kitchen.

I frowned and looked around.

"Is that the breaker? Why would the power be out? There's no storm."

After turning off the flame on the stove so there wasn't an incident, I went to search for the breaker.

Fear coated my tongue as I found it and saw all of the breakers turned to OFF.

I looked around, trying to figure out how that could have happened, and then something struck me upside the head. I fell, my head hitting the tile floor, and someone grabbed my ankle.

I looked up, tasting blood in my mouth, as I saw Brayden.

"You weren't supposed to fucking be here. What the hell are you doing here?" he snapped, and I kicked out, connecting with his knee and he let go.

Panic surged, and I crawled around him, staggering to my feet while my head pounded. I slid on a dryer sheet, smacked my shoulder into the doorway, and kept going. My feet slapped the tile in the kitchen as I ran towards my phone, but then Brayden pulled my hair, tugging me back. I flew back into him, my shoulders slamming into his chest, and he growled, keeping me tight.

"Don't you fucking dare move. You think you can do this? You think you can destroy my family? I see you fucking my brother. Using him to hurt us. Well, now, I'm going to show the Wilders what happens when you hurt us. We hurt you right back."

I froze for just a moment, afraid of what he'd do, before I pushed at him, not wanting him to touch me.

"Don't you fucking dare," I growled, knowing I was

strong. I moved, trying to run for the front door, but Brayden was bigger and faster.

It didn't matter what techniques Evan had taught me. Brayden was big. He slammed me to the floor, and I kicked out, screaming, hoping someone would hear me. But we were so far out. There wasn't a house near enough to hear my screams. Dear God, someone needed to hear me. And then Brayden was over me. He pushed at me and slapped my face.

"Don't you fucking dare." He kneed my gut, slapped me again, and I pushed back, screaming, fighting.

"No. No."

"You think you're too good for me? You're fucking a Wilder. You can have me."

We were at the stove, the power out, nothing around me, so I kicked out and hit him between the legs, my knee smashing into his balls. He let out a sharp gasp and then tried to reach for my throat, connecting and squeezing. I pushed at him and scrambled up. When he came for me, ignoring his own pain, I slid on my own blood and reached for the pot on the stove.

My hand burned on the metal, but I lifted it anyway and sloshed hot—but unfortunately not boiling—water on Brayden's chest. He shouted, touching the wetness.

"You bitch. You're going to pay for that."

He kept coming. I ran, trying to get away. Even

burnt, even hurt, he kept coming. He gripped my hair again and slammed me to the ground.

My elbow and my head slammed into the floor, and I cried out, tears mixing with my own blood.

"You're going to pay for that," he snarled, his face red and splotchy, and all I could do was hope to hell someone heard me.

I would not go down without fighting. *I would not.*

And then the door slammed open, and Evan was there, and oddly LJ was right behind him. Evan saw Brayden on top of me and growled, snarling. LJ did the same, and then I couldn't focus. I saw double, bile rising in my throat as I turned to the side and threw up.

I didn't know if it was stress from what happened or if I had a concussion.

LJ was ripping his brother off of him, and Evan was holding me, keeping me close.

I shied away from him, scared, and I saw the hurt on his face, but I couldn't focus, couldn't breathe.

"You fucking asshole," LJ shouted as he punched his brother. And then I was curled into a ball on the floor as Evan turned towards Brayden.

I saw death in his eyes, and I knew if I didn't stop them, they would kill him.

And I didn't want Brayden dead. Not because he

deserved to live, but because LJ and Evan didn't deserve what could happen if they killed him.

"Stop. I need help," I rasped, and Evan turned immediately and pulled me close. This time I didn't flinch away, I just let him hold me as Brayden hit the floor, unconscious, and LJ shook, pulling out his phone.

"I'm calling 911."

"I need to call my brothers," Evan whispered.

But I didn't hear them. I didn't do anything.

I just let my tears fall, and I cried, grateful they had been there.

As the sirens got closer, and as the Wilders and others arrived, I cried and shut myself off, and let Evan hold me.

Chapter Seventeen

Evan

"Evan. Evan."

I ignored Eli's growl. Knowing if I spoke to him right then, I would probably do something I regretted.

My hands shook, and I tried to catch my breath, tried to think.

But for the past two days, all I could do was growl and pace.

Two days of speaking to cops, of watching them ransack my house as they went through everything

collecting evidence from the assault. Two days of waiting by Kendall's bedside as doctors looked over her and put stitches on her forehead and the back of her head. Two days of pretending that I was the strong one as Kendall broke in my arms.

Two days where I lied to myself day in and day out.

But those two days had been the longest and shortest of my life.

And if I turned to my brothers just then, I wasn't sure how I would react. Because it was all I could do not to rush back to the cabin where Kendall was sleeping and hold her and never let her go.

She didn't need me breaking just then. She needed me to be as strong as I had pretended to be for these past two days. So I would. And I would lie. But I could not turn around.

"Evan." I froze, that voice not one of my brothers, but one that I could either hate or understand.

Which I would choose was the question.

"I'm not in the mood, LJ," I said after a moment and leaned against the post on the porch.

We were at East's cabin now, his small porch just big enough for two rocking chairs. I stood at the bottom of the steps, not wanting to sit down, since getting up after a long week of not taking care of myself would be impossible without help. My leg ached, and it had nothing to do with phantom pain and all to do with how I jerked it around when I was throwing myself down to protect Kendall.

"I know you're not in the mood, but I've got to talk to you. Then, after this, you can never talk to me again, if that's what you want."

I looked over my shoulder at the man with dark circles under his eyes, his hair disheveled, and saw the pain in his gaze.

"You look like shit."

LJ's lips twitched, and I had a feeling that all five of my brothers were inside East's small cabin, their noses pressed against the window as they listened in on this conversation. It didn't matter. I was done.

"I'm sorry," LJ said after a moment, and I blinked up at him.

"What do you mean you're sorry? You don't have anything to be sorry about, LJ." And that was the truth of it. Maybe the angrier version of myself, the person that hadn't fallen in love with Kendall again, would've blamed him.

Kendall, who'd seen the good in me, and it calmed me.

Maybe not enough, but just the right amount.

"My brother...fuck. I knew my brother was an

egotistical asshole. I knew he'd do anything he could to get what he wanted. But I didn't know he was violent." LJ leaned against the other pillar, staring down at his hands.

"You didn't know at all?" I asked, and LJ stared blankly at me. "Again. I'm not blaming you. The more we got to know you, LJ, the more we knew you were not your brother."

"He and my dad wanted Dodge Ranch to be the best place, a destination for people, because that's what our family did. My dad may be a jerk about it, may be underhanded, but he was never violent towards us. Brayden, though? I can't even imagine how he thought what he did would help anything."

I was the one who looked down at my hands that time.

"He was going through my files, trying to see if he could get anything on the resort and the winery."

LJ nodded tightly. "That's what the cops said after they questioned me."

"Elijah said they had you for a few hours. You okay?"

LJ shook his head. "No, but I'd stay for hours longer if that meant we hadn't seen what we had. Because that would mean Kendall hadn't gone through what she did."

Bile slid up my throat and I swallowed hard, looking away from the other man.

"I don't even keep those files in my house. They're all up at the winery, or in the cloud, or maybe even with Elijah. I wouldn't keep anything here that he could have used to take our business. Instead, I left the woman that I love here and thought she was safe."

"The concussion was mild, right?" LJ asked, and I nodded tightly.

"The concussion was mild, and she has bruises down her face, sides, arms. But she and the doctor swear that was it."

Nausea roiled, thinking about what else the other man could have done. The taunting and fear had shaken her. That's what I saw in her eyes. And that's why I was here, giving her space while she was with the girls, resting. And I would find a way to do something to protect her. Because I sure as hell hadn't been enough yet.

"I don't know where to go from here. Other than I'm oddly glad that I was here to talk with Eli," LJ said after a minute.

I looked up at him and frowned. "You pulled him off of her."

"You would've done it, too, but you went to her, and I tried to beat the shit out of my brother."

He said that so dryly it shocked me.

"What's going to happen now?" I asked, trying to breathe, yet my chest felt too tight.

"I don't know," LJ said after a minute. "I know he hired a lawyer, and my dad is helping. But I'm not part of that decision. Or part of any of that."

"Fuck, man."

"Pretty much. I hope they put him away for a long time. That he gets the help that he needs." LJ sighed. "That's *my* brother. My fucking brother did that. My dad is not talking to me, and thinks it's all a misunderstanding. As if he could use his words and cajoling to get Brayden out of this."

"It's not going to fucking happen."

"No. We were there. Kendall's account and the evidence are going to help. I just wish there was another way to keep her safe."

"He cut the power to the fucking house, Evan," Everett said from behind me, and I turned to see my brothers come outside. Everett was rubbing his temple, and I knew he hadn't slept at all for these past two days. I wasn't sure any of my brothers had slept, but Everett needed more sleep than most of us because of his injury.

"I'm going to head out," LJ said. "Dad is not at the ranch, and he has his staff working on things, but I guess it's ingrained in me that a Dodge always needs to be there."

"I thought you weren't working with them anymore?" Eli asked, scowling.

LJ's gaze was bleak as he shrugged. "I'm not. But I don't want our staff, who have done nothing wrong, to be harmed because of my brother and my father. So I'll figure out how to help them, and then I'll be back to talk. Because I don't know what else to do." And with that, LJ shrugged and walked away, and I just watched after him, knowing that if he felt as bad as he did, if he had felt one inch of what I was feeling, he must feel as if the world was ending.

"Do you want to talk?" Everett asked, and I scowled at my younger brother.

"No, I don't want to fucking talk. I want to go back in time and fix this. But just like everything else, I can't."

"It's not your fault," Elijah whispered, and I whirled on him.

"I left her alone."

"In your locked fucking house," he snarled.

"I'll be changing all the locks again. Making them from stronger stuff. Because fuck this," East growled, before he stomped away and headed towards the shed near his house.

"I need to go back to the main house. Naomi and Amos are handling most things, but they can't do it all."

I nodded as Elliot walked away, and Elijah followed after saying his goodbyes, because somebody needed to be at the winery.

They had all stopped everything for Kendall, as was only right, and yet I felt like I wasn't doing anything right.

"Just stop. Just fucking stop. I'm just done. I couldn't protect her before, and I couldn't protect her now."

"What do you mean by before?" Everett asked softly.

I swallowed hard and figured while I was here, I might as well tell them everything.

"Do you remember Ward? Keegan?"

Everett froze as Eli nodded tightly.

"We remember. We remember when you almost died then. And then again when you lost your leg. We remember it all, Evan."

"Back then now, it was the three of us. Because we were all growing in different directions, us Wilder brothers. We all needed to. To grow up. And we didn't get to be stationed in the same place."

"I know. It's one of the hardest decisions I ever had to make to leave you guys the first time."

"And then we followed," Everett added.

"And then we followed," I repeated. "But Keegan, Ward, and I? They were my brothers, too."

"Good. It's good you had them," Everett whispered.

"And I lost them. But we made a pact. That we would take care of the women that we loved. Because they were at my wedding. That whirlwind wedding that happened out of nowhere. And you guys couldn't make it because you got, what, two minutes notice?" I asked, a hollow laugh rattling my chest.

"We know."

"We would've been there. Somehow," Everett whispered.

"Eliza was the only one disappointed. But that was just because she wanted to be in the wedding in a pretty dress," Eli teased. "And then she lost her husband. Just like we lost everyone else. But those guys? We promised that we would take care of our women if we were killed in action. And I still try to help Britney and Lacey when I can. But they don't need my help anymore. They want to hear updates about my life even though I don't fucking have any. But they don't need my help."

"Is that why you left Kendall?" Everett asked, his voice low, and I stiffened.

"Yeah," I croaked out, and Eli cursed under his breath before he began to pace on the small porch.

"You fucking idiot," Eli grumbled.

"I didn't want to make her a widow. So I broke her heart instead. We're fixing that, or at least I thought we were. But now? I don't know. I lost everything before. Keegan, Ward, my future. And then I lost my fucking leg. Everything has changed over and over again. Every time I look towards the future and make plans, things pivot and I can't find my way."

"But you are. Don't you understand?" Everett asked. "You are finding your way."

"I almost lost Kendall. After all of that, I almost lost her."

"But you didn't," Everett whispered. "Go to her. All of us, more than most, know that life is short. We know that we could lose everything, but why can't we live? Why can't we just look to our future and try to live? Go to her. She needs you now, more than ever. She's going to be okay, Evan. But don't let her think you're going to walk away again. She doesn't deserve that."

Fear coated my tongue. "I don't want that. I don't want her to think that. I'm not fucking going away. If anything, I'm going to stay closer."

"Then fucking go to her," Eli snarled.

I looked at them, nodded tightly, and grabbed my phone from the bench next to me. "I'm leaving. I have to go see her."

"Of course you do. Just remember it wasn't your fault then, and it isn't now."

I looked at both of my brothers and swallowed hard, and then headed towards Kendall. I didn't know if I could fix this, but walking away wasn't an option. So instead, I walked towards her. Making the first good decision I had in days.

Chapter Eighteen

Kendall

"I'm not good at making this soup," Alexis said as she scowled over the pot on the stove. "I'm just reheating soup from the freezer. You would think I would be better at this."

That made my lips twitch, just like I knew Alexis wanted.

"How did you mess it up? You shouldn't have been able to."

"Oh, it doesn't take her long to mess that up." Maddie leaned forward, her lips tilting to a smile.

"Hey. I can cook. I'm a good cook. Maybe I'm not a *you* kind of cook, but I'm decently good."

"So she says," Joy teased, and I looked at the three women in my small borrowed living room and smiled.

"You guys are sweet. Thank you for being here. Though I know you guys have some work to do."

"We may have work, but hanging out with you is a lot more fun."

"Oh really?" I asked, laughing.

"Of course."

"I'm getting soup out of the deal," Joy put in. "Maybe soup that's going to make me ill later, but totally soup."

"I heard that," Alexis snapped, though she was laughing. "And it's not burnt. It's just taking a while to all blend together."

"Do you need to add water?" I asked as I tried to lever myself up off the couch.

Maddie gave me a look and pointed her finger at me. "Sit."

"I'm fine."

"You sit right down, and we will bring you food."

Joy smiled softly. "You have to do what she says."

"I'm fine. Really. The bruises are fading, I'm comfortable, and the stitches aren't that bad." I wasn't lying about any of it. I was fine.

Yes, I had bruises down my face, shoulders, and back, but it could have been so much worse. A shudder went through me, and I swallowed hard. So much worse.

Brayden might have hurt me, but Evan didn't scar me. The only thing that could scar me is if Evan didn't come back.

"I just find it odd that we're in this cabin and not at my house, or even Evan's."

"Evan's needs to be cleaned up," Alexis said, her voice soft. "You know that."

"I do—one hundred percent. And I get it. And I hope that he lets me help with the cleanup. I think it'll be good for me." I nodded tightly as the girls gave me a look to see if I was lying. "No, really. It'll help. I don't want this to be a thing. I don't want me to be stressed out all the time and worried about having a flashback. He didn't hurt me in the way that you guys are thinking. You do know that, right? He didn't touch me."

"Thank God for that," Alexis said as she swallowed hard. "But he did hurt you. And I want to find him and strangle him, and I realize that reacting to violence with violence isn't the way to do things, and yet that's all I want to do."

"I want to be able to go into that house and not see my fear. And I realize that I'm at this cabin instead of at my house because everyone wanted me to be close. And we have to keep the resort and winery up and running. And I want to go back to work, as soon as I can hold a pan without freaking out." They all stared at me, alarm in their gaze, and I cringed. "I just mean that my shoulder hurts. A pan saved me. I'm going to always love pans of water." I knew I was trying to lighten things up, but I wasn't sure what else to say. Yes, I had been scared, but I was going to be okay. I was going to talk it out. And as long as Evan came back, I would be fine. He just needed to come back.

"You fought. Probably far harder than I could," Joy added.

"Evan taught me how to protect myself, but I feel like I need to take classes. You know?"

"I can make that happen," Maddie put in. "Because I only know basic self-defense. And I realize that it may seem an odd thing to say right now, but let's do that. Be proactive." She cringed. "Unless that's insensitive."

"I'm the one that brought it up," I said. "Let's be proactive, because I'm okay. Brayden is behind bars, his dad isn't bothering us anymore, and LJ feels like shit, but he's going to fix things. We are all going to be okay."

"And I'm not going to ruin the soup," Alexis added, and we all laughed, and I was grateful for it. My body may ache, but my soul wouldn't. I wouldn't let this define me. No matter what happened next.

We ate our soup, and then everyone left to go back to their jobs or their men. I sat back and waited for Evan to come home. He said he would, and he had to be on his way soon. I also had needed some time alone, and I was grateful the girls gave me that time.

My phone rang, and I nearly jumped for it, then remembered that everything hurt. I looked at the readout and tensed at the sight of my mom's name.

I let out a deep breath and then answered. "Hello, Mom."

"Kendall. Are you okay? Evan called."

I froze, but I shouldn't have been surprised. I had a complicated relationship with my parents, and Evan, above all people, knew that. I might not like them all the time, but they did love me. We just weren't good at communicating, and they weren't good at figuring out my needs. Or where I fit into the family.

"I'm okay."

"It doesn't seem that way. And to think, it was the Dodge's son? I'm so sorry. Is there anything your father and I can do? I know that we always fight when we're near, but your dad and I want to be there for you."

She kept talking, and I answered her questions, but I

didn't need them there. I had the Wilders and my girls. I had the family that I had made.

My relationship was never going to be easy with my parents. And the fact that she hadn't mentioned my brother just meant that he didn't care. But that was okay with me. I didn't need my brother in my life, but the fact that my mother had reached out? That was progress.

I wasn't the person that I had been when I had first married Evan. I wasn't the daughter that they had always wanted. But she called to check on me.

She was sorry. And it seemed like she was pushing the Dodges out of her life.

I had to count that for something.

"I'll let you rest. But if you want something, you know I can order food. I can't really cook it," Mom teased, and I laughed. "Well, I'm glad I got my cooking skills from someone else then," I teased.

"That is true. Though it wasn't me or your father. Not quite sure where it came from, but I'm glad for it. You're an amazing cook, sweetie."

I wasn't sure exactly who this woman was, but she did not sound like my mother. However, I wasn't going to start a fight, so I let her continue to make sure I was okay, and then she hung up after saying goodbye, neither one of us saying we loved each other. We didn't really use those words.

Come to think of it, the last person I truly said it to was Evan. It had been over eight years. I still hadn't told him now.

But I should. Only, I was afraid that if I did now, he would think it was because of the attack and not because I really did, so I wouldn't yet. As long as he showed up, then I would be okay.

And, as if I had summoned him, he walked through the door, his gaze intense as he studied my face.

"You're still awake."

"It's in the middle of the afternoon, and I slept for thirteen hours yesterday. I have a book, a recipe tablet, and I'm just sitting here. I'm okay." I met his gaze, determined. "I'm okay."

He swallowed hard, locked the door behind him, and then came to sit next to me on the couch. But he didn't touch me. I just wanted him to hold me. And maybe that was wrong, to want to rely and lean on someone, but I hadn't for so long. Maybe it was okay that I did.

"Your bruises are turning a different color," he whispered.

"They do that," I said as I reached up to touch my face, then thought better of it.

"Mine always go this weird lime green color, and I never understood why," he added.

"I guess we can compare bruises." I leaned forward and brushed my fingers along his knuckles. "Are you okay?"

"You shouldn't be the one asking that."

"No, maybe I should be. I was scared, Evan. But I knew you would come," I added as his gaze went dark.

"I was almost too late."

"But you weren't too late. You showed up, and so did LJ." I winced. "I'm sorry for bringing him up."

"He helped save you. I'm never going to hate him for that."

"Oh."

"Yeah, oh. I've done a lot of wrong things in my life. Leaving you, for one. But I don't want to make any more wrong decisions. So, I'm here, Kendall. Anything you need. I'm here."

I started to cry at that. He scrambled, lifting me oh so carefully into his lap. "Did I hurt you?"

I shook my head and leaned into him. "No. You don't hurt me, Evan."

"Good. Let me just hold you."

"Yes. That's what I need. Because I'll be okay, Evan."

"And I won't leave. I'm here."

It was as if he had heard the words in my mind without me even having to say them.

"I don't want you to go."

"And I'm not going anywhere. You're mine, Kendall." We sat there for a long while, both of us just leaning into one another, no words needed, until he let out a breath, and I looked up at him. "What is it?"

"I think it's time we go see Lacey and Britney."

I froze, hope and relief and worry all rolled into one inside me. "Are you sure?"

"I'm sure. Britney emailed a couple of weeks ago with photos of the kids, and I figured maybe we could go down there. I don't know, is that closure or just futures? I don't know anymore. But I'm tired of doing things without you, Kendall. I'm tired of worrying about what the past brought us, and maybe it's time to look to the future. Because I almost lost you. I'm not fucking doing it again."

Tears fell, but this time they were happy, and I leaned forward and brushed my lips against his.

"Okay. I'd love to see them again, as long as I'm with you, Evan. We're going to be okay. Together."

He cupped my face and kissed me softly, and then he held me, and I was nearly asleep when I heard him whisper one last thing and I knew I was safe.

Home.

"Together."

Chapter Nineteen

Evan

In the two weeks since the attack, nothing had changed on the legal front. But those things took time. Brayden was formally charged, and other things were in motion, but we were still waiting for everything else. Kendall was back in the kitchen, and I was at the winery. We were working long hours, trying to stay focused on what we could.

Bliss hadn't come back to us, but I wasn't sure they would. I knew the sons were trying, but old man Bliss was still firmly in Dodge's camp. Even if the family was disgraced. I wasn't even sure I wanted to work with Bliss at this point, but it was just something in the background as we focused on everything else.

Kendall had indeed helped cleanup my cabin as she wanted to, but we were staying at her place, not mine. I wasn't sure I *wanted* to stay in mine, even though Kendall said she was ready. But it was nice, the two of us together.

And that was exactly what we were doing right then. Staying together as we drove across the state, outside the Dallas area, to go see Lacey and Britney.

"How long have they been here?" Kendall asked after a moment, and I looked over at her before putting my eyes back on the road, tangling my fingers with hers over the center console.

"Four years or so, I think."

"I was trying to remember from our emails, but I haven't been as good as I should when it came to keeping up."

"Same here. I've tried, but they wanted to move on, and I couldn't...before."

She squeezed my hand, and I swallowed hard. "You can move on while still remembering. That's something that I'm not that great at."

"Same. But we're working on it." I looked at her again before the GPS told us to take an exit.

"It'll be so weird to see them. The kids must be how old now?"

"The kids we knew are around eight and ten."

Kendall sucked in a breath. "It's so weird to think that we could have kids those ages too."

I swallowed hard. "This is probably not the right time to ask this. Maybe it is. Do you ever regret not having kids in those two years?"

She was silent for so long I was afraid I had said something wrong. Fuck, I wasn't sure I wanted to know her answer.

"Sometimes, because what an amazing feat that would be to have a little eight- or ten-year-old right now. To see them grow, but we weren't ready before. Britney and Lacey were. Their relationships with Ward and Keegan were far different than ours."

"You're right."

"And we had wanted to wait. We had purposefully decided we were going to. While we waited, our lives changed. We needed to become the people we are now in order for us to find each other again. And while it would have been so sweet and amazing to have a child then, we needed to be who we are."

I smiled as I turned down the road. "Again, you're right."

"It doesn't always feel like I'm right," she said with a

laugh. "A lot of times it feels like I'm just blowing smoke, but we weren't ready for kids then, and you staying for children, me staying for kids, that wouldn't have been fair to anyone."

I squeezed her hand again, sucking in a breath. "We just need to do better."

"We will."

I didn't ask the obvious question, if either one of us were ready for children now. I wasn't sure we were, nor was I sure it was the right time. I knew she had wanted kids in the past, when she was ready. But when was that time?

It wasn't like we were past the age of kids. Hell, my family was just now starting to settle down. If we wanted children, we could have them. But, one thing at a time. Facing our past was a good way to start.

We followed the directions and pulled into a nice subdivision, with two- and three-car garages and children playing in the front yards with adults watching and laughing.

"This seems like a nice place."

"It does. Sometimes I forget that so much time has passed, and yet sometimes it feels like it's been ages."

"That's exactly how I feel. Eight years is a long time. And yet, here we are."

We pulled up to a two-story house, with one car in

the large driveway. I turned off the car, squeezed Kendall's hand again, and I looked over at her.

"Are you ready?"

"As ready as I'll ever be."

We got out of the car, and before we could fully get everything out of the backseat, a familiar woman with blonde hair was running towards us.

"You're here. I'm so happy that you're here. And together. Oh, my God!" Britney said, laughing, her blonde hair flowing around her. Another familiar blonde followed suit, and I laughed, unable to help myself.

I held out my arms and they both slammed into me. I staggered back, gritting my teeth slightly since my foot wasn't where it needed to be, and they each pulled back.

"Crap. Are you okay? I did that to Dylan once, and his prosthetic fell right off his knee. I could have slapped myself. Are you okay?"

I smiled at the other woman and remembered that her new husband had lost his foot in a motorcycle accident when he was a teenager. Neither one of their husbands were in the military, and I didn't blame them. I had gotten out, after all, so had the rest of my family. Losing a love of your life like they had changed their priorities, and I was grateful that they were here.

"Come on in."

"We've got food," Kendall said with a laugh. "I'm sorry. Can't help it."

"I'm just so happy you're here. And together!" Lacey added, and they hugged Kendall close, and then they were unpacking the baked goods and other dishes that Kendall had made and stored in specially marked containers. We had presents for the kids, and even though we were only there for the day—the long drive was going to be hell on us later that night—this trip was worth it. With a big wedding coming up, we couldn't take more than a day for this trip, but today was what we had needed. At least, I hoped so.

We were introduced to both Dylan and Ashton, both men loud, rambunctious, and fit both women to a T. They were good men who treated their women like they were goddesses, and I knew that both Ward and Keegan would be happy for them.

The children were out in the back, and when they were introduced to their Uncle Evan and Aunt Kendall Wilder, there was a little hitch in my throat, and Kendall wrapped her arms around my waist.

"We're going to be here more. I promise," she whispered, and I kissed the top of her head.

"Yeah. We will."

Britney grinned. "Come on over. We have cupcakes

to start with. As Ward always said, dessert before our meal is sometimes what we need."

It did my heart good to hear both of them talking about their late husbands. The children's fathers. Their new husbands fit right into the family and spoke of Ward and Keegan as if they had known them as well. Everyone had moved on but hadn't forgotten.

My problem was I had languished in the past and hadn't moved on.

But, as we spoke of who we were then and where we were now, it felt as if this was the moment that I had needed. The moment *we* had needed.

"I'm just so happy that you guys are together again," Britney said as she clapped her hands.

Lacey rolled her eyes as both of their husbands laughed, keeping an eye on the kids. "What? I know we should be all quiet and respectful of your new relationship and trying to tiptoe around things, but hell. It's good for us to talk about it. Because you guys were amazing together. I'm just glad that you guys are back together. And eventually, I'm going to need all that story," she said as she looked past me and directly at Kendall.

"We'll do wine," Britney added, the two of them inseparable as ever.

"I can totally do that, and when you come down to

the resort and winery, you can meet the girls down there. Maddie can tell us exactly what wine to drink."

"Oh, we'll be staying there," Lacey said.

Britney nodded. "I've been looking at your place. It looks great. Perfect for a weekend out, or whatever."

I cleared my throat. "Kids are welcome as well. My younger brother usually is fantastic at figuring out perfect activities for everybody involved."

"I still can't believe you're a wine connoisseur." Lacey smiled. "It feels good. As if we're all finding our places."

"I'd like to think so. We're trying. One day at a time."

Lacey looked over her shoulder at the kids playing in the yard, out of earshot. Then she let out a breath and looked towards us. "Losing Keegan was the hardest thing I've ever gone through. I know that there are other hard things that people go through, but for me, losing him meant that I had to suddenly be a single mom, no longer connected to the military, on the outside looking in. But I had you, Evan. And I had Britney. And I had you, Kendall."

"We had each other," Britney whispered, she squeezed her hand.

"I'm sorry that I wasn't around as much, that I left the way that I did," Kendall whispered, and I hated myself right then, but Kendall leaned forward and kissed me on the cheek. "It's okay," she whispered.

"We all had to figure out who we were, but we've all kept in touch. Maybe not perfectly, but it has worked out."

"I mean, in a way that made sense of some semblance of healing," Britney said after a moment.

"You guys found each other again, and we found happiness, too. We lost something back then, but we found something as well." Each of the women looked at their husbands, and each of those men smiled softly at them. I knew without a doubt that both women still loved their late husbands, because grief was everlasting but changed in its ebbs and flows. I still considered them my brothers, but I loved my blood brothers too. There was enough in all of us to be connected to all those parts of our worlds.

"Anyway," Britney said as she wiped her tears away, "Happy things. Because we can dwell in sadness, or we can just remember it and know that we're allowed to be happy. So, you guys are here, together, and I love this for you both. Seriously, I'm just so happy." She started clapping, and I laughed as Kendall beamed, and we spoke of harder things and happier things. The kids came in, and we got to know them a bit more, and I sighed, held Kendall close, and knew that this was good for us. We weren't saying goodbye, because this family would always be part of ours, but now it wasn't two halves of a whole. Instead, it was one part of many that became us.

Later that night, we piled in the car and made our way home. It was nearly five hours between, but it was worth the drive.

"I'm exhausted, but I'm so glad that we got to see them," Kendall said as she maneuvered off the highway on our exit. I had driven us there and part of the way back, but my leg was hurting, so she finished the trip. It was nice having someone to take turns with, everything just fell right in line.

"It was good. I wish I could have stayed longer. Gotten a hotel or something."

"True, we just have that meeting."

I grumbled. "I don't want a meeting. I just want this Bliss thing to be over."

"It will be over soon, and then we can eat, make love, and drink wine."

"All in that order?" I asked, laughing.

"I don't know. Seeing those kids there? Got me thinking of all kinds of things."

I froze. "Really?"

"Too soon?"

"Baby. I feel like I've known you all my life. You say when, and I'm there."

"It'll probably be a little harder than that, but, I don't know, things feel good." I squeezed her hand, my heart far too full. Something I would never have thought before this. "It does feel good."

We pulled off onto the next street and made our way towards the Wilder Resort when headlights flashed behind us.

"Why do people use their high beams?"

"No fucking clue. It's fucking annoying."

"Right? But they're coming up fast, Evan. What do I do?"

I turned, ice sliding in my veins. "Pull off the road, let them pass you."

"There's not a lot of space here, and there's a curve coming up."

"Shit," I growled, and then the car got closer, and metal screeched, and there was a scream, and I couldn't do anything. Kendall was the one behind the wheel. All I could do was sit there and hope to hell that we could stop the car. I gripped the steering wheel with her, keeping it steady as we went off the road, my teeth rattling in my skull as we hit the embankment and spun two circles in the mud.

"Evan!" Kendall called out as we finally pulled to a stop, facing the opposite way, dust and debris all in the air.

"Are you okay? Baby, are you okay?"

She nodded, her face pale, her eyes wide. "I'm not hurt. Are you?"

"I'm fine." I patted myself, making sure that wasn't a lie. "I'm fine. What the fuck?"

"Was he drunk? Who was that?"

I finally looked up, saw the truck face down in a ditch. A familiar truck, and cursed under my breath. "Call 911. It wasn't an accident."

I jimmied open my door, got out, and ignored the ache in my leg as Kendall scrambled behind me.

"Baby. Stop it. Don't go over there."

"Oh, I'm going over there," I snarled as Kendall began to dial 911, but she didn't stay back. No, she was right by my side.

But since Dodge was in the truck, pinned to his seat by the airbag, I didn't feel like we were in any danger.

No, the other man couldn't move with the way that he was situated, and there was blood seeping slowly from a wound in his head.

But he could still speak, the asshole.

"Fuck you! You're ruining my life. You've ruined our family."

I just stared at Dodge, at the ruined truck and the ruined man, and I didn't feel the urge to pull him out of the vehicle and beat the shit out of him. Instead, I just stared at him, at the mess of his own making, and turned away and faced the woman that I loved.

"Baby. I love you so fucking much. Are you okay?"

Her eyes widened, and she nodded, the phone still to her ear. "I love you, too," she whispered, the words I'd been waiting to hear for eons finally piercing my soul. I leaned down and took her mouth and then looked over her, the high beams of our car highlighting her so I could see if she was hurt anywhere.

"Ambulance and cops are on their way."

"Good. And I'll be damned if a member of the Dodge family hurts us again."

I held her close as sirens rang and other cars stopped on the side of the road. Eli and Elijah were there, Everett coming in right after, and I knew they had questions, and we would have to talk with them. But right then, I just needed to hold Kendall and hope to hell she was okay for real. Because I had almost lost her again, to another fucking Dodge.

But in the end, it wouldn't matter. Because she was okay, she had to be okay.

And she was mine.

Chapter Twenty

Kendall

"My poor car," I said after a minute, looking up at Evan.

He scowled down at me, then wrapped his arm around my shoulder. "We'll get you a new one. A better one."

"Nothing was better than my car. I'm going to miss it."

"I'm going to get you a tank," Eli grumbled, and I looked over at the Wilder brothers, their women, and the family that we were making. We sat in the employee lounge area of the winery, all of us tangled together, exhausted and still confused about everything that had happened.

It had been a long night and an even longer day, going through police questioning and getting my car out of the ditch.

We had also had to prep for a wedding and pretend that we weren't dealing with the ramifications of what the Dodges had done.

Oh, there were whispers, everybody knew what was going on, but we didn't want our clients and guests to understand it because we wanted them to be able to enjoy their day. It was an odd dichotomy, and I wasn't sure we got the balance right. That afternoon, I had been able to finally get back in the kitchen and just pretend for a bit.

Now we were all together, exhausted, and going over things regarding the Dodges so we could end our day with hopefully fewer questions.

"A tank could be nice, but will it have room for all of my catering and food in the back?" I asked, leaning into Evan. His warmth sank into my bones, and I let out a breath, knowing he was my rock, my hope. Just like I was his.

We were a partnership. Something we should have been in the beginning and were now finding our way through.

"I don't want you to ever leave this room. Or my side."

I patted his thigh and shook my head. "You were in the car too, mister. You were in just as much danger as me. But together, we got the car off to the side of the road. Even though now my car is totaled, we're going to be fine. Damn it."

"Hear! Hear!" Elijah said as he held up his wine glass. Joy wasn't with him, as she was on a work trip out of town, but Alexis lay next to Elijah on a small couch, and Maddie was there as well, with Sandy having gone home after picking up some of my shifts lately. Our new hires were doing well, but it was still putting a lot on Sandy's shoulders. But I was back. I wasn't going to force her to do too much anymore.

"So, Dodge is going to jail for attempted murder, right?" Alexis asked, confused. "Are they going to take it down to a misdemeanor of drunk driving? Or is that a felony? This is why I'm not a lawyer."

I snorted, even as my stomach rolled. "I only know what I learned from *Law and Order*, and it's not much."

"Honestly, the only thing I learned from *Law and Order* is if you recognize an actor, they're the bad guy," Maddie put in, and I laughed. I was so grateful I could laugh right then as the Wilder brothers continued to discuss what the ramifications would be.

"They have him on drunk driving and endangerment, but I'm not sure what else they're going to put on there. He could have killed you." Everett scowled. "I just don't know what else they can take him for. Especially with him railing against you guys. Still."

"With the way that the tire tracks are, and from where the collision was, they're not going to be able to say it's your fault," Eli put in.

"And I guess the good thing is Brayden is going to be in jail for a lot longer than he thought," East added, and I froze, turning to the other man. Everyone did the same, and he blushed.

"You didn't hear?" East asked, and I shook my head. "He stabbed a guy in jail. With a shiv and everything. He wasn't even locked up in prison, just jail at that point, but he stabbed someone."

My hands shook and I swallowed hard. Evan seemed to know I was feeling every emotion at once and squeezed me tightly.

"And thanks to our society, him doing that is probably going to get him more time than he would for assault, right?" Alexis asked and winced. "I'm sorry."

"No, the longer he's in jail, the better. I just feel bad for LJ." I bit my lip, my mind heavy.

The men in the room scowled at me, but it was Evan who leaned to the side and kissed my temple. "We'll make sure he's okay. He helped us. We're not going to let him flounder."

"You're a good man, Evan Wilder," I whispered as I kissed him softly.

"Well, we don't have any answers yet, and we won't until the law takes care of it. But they have evidence, and we've protected our family." Eli looked at us all and nodded tightly. "That's all we can do. Other than making sure that Wilder stays on top of its game and continues doing its best. We are all doing it as a family. And that's all that matters."

He held up his wine glass, and I held up my water, others holding up various beverages.

"To the Wilders," Maddie said and smiled. She was the only one here not truly connected to the Wilders by a relationship, but she was family.

"To the Wilders," Evan whispered, and I leaned against his shoulder and touched my glass to his. I knew that we would find our way. Finally.

By the time we went back to his cabin, I was tired and ready to sleep.

"Are you sure you're okay staying here? We can stay in any other open room on this property. Or hell, I'll drive you home."

I shook my head. "We've been sleeping in three different beds in rotation, and I kind of just want to stay in one place. With you. I just want to be with you, Evan. Wherever it may be."

He looked at me and cupped my face. Everything that happened in the past few months felt like it was twisting in my mind, changing and making things difficult, but at the same time, the sense of clarity that opened up by just being by his side, knowing that we were trusting one another with each other's hearts and everything else made it worth it.

"I think while you say this place doesn't hurt to see, I don't know if it's big enough for the two of us."

I froze, confused. "What do you mean?"

"These places were always supposed to be temporary. For each of us. That way, we brothers could find a sense of home before we branched out to who we needed to be. I don't know how long Elijah will be at his place before he and Joy move in together. Eli and Alexis already have their own place. I want to be with you. I don't want us to rotate between homes. I don't want to let you go, Kendall."

"I don't want you to let me go either," I whispered, my heart beating so quickly it echoed in my ears.

"So, what do you say we make our future together? We find a house that's perfect for us. Whether it be your current one or a new one. Something that we could have for our future."

"Evan, what are you saying?" I whispered, tears flowing. And then he took my hands, and I swallowed hard, my hands shaking. "Evan."

"We married in Vegas, with love, an instant attraction. We married because of our potential, but without a foundation. We built part of that foundation before, but now I want to secure it. I want to continue to find our path together. You know I'm not great with words," he continued, and I shook my head.

"You're doing pretty well right now," I blurted, then put my hands over my mouth, shaking.

He just smiled at me, and though I knew this moment would mean forever, I could barely breathe.

"I love you, Kendall. I've loved you for so many years now. It's like this aching moment of my soul that will never go away. I've loved you for longer than I've known, and I'm never walking away from you. No matter what happens, no matter what we face, you're mine. Just like I'm yours." He opened a velvet box he pulled from somewhere, and my hands shook as I lowered them, my eyes filling with tears. Nestled within the velvet were two rings. One familiar, the small diamond winking up at me. I couldn't believe what I was looking at.

"How did you get that?"

"When I walked away, you threw it. But I picked it

up." He let out a shaky breath. "And I've kept it all this time. Because I shouldn't have left, but I have it, to remind us of who we were before, but I have this other one to remind us of who we can be together now."

Next to that small ring that held so many memories was a larger one, with a square-cut diamond surrounded by yellow diamonds, in the most gorgeous setting I'd ever seen. Not modern, and not too traditional. But unique, and something all our own.

He cleared his throat. "I thought we could do something with the smaller one, or you can wear it on your necklace. I know you don't always wear rings while you're cooking, but we could do something. I have a chain too, but it didn't fit well in the box."

I looked up at him then, tears freely flowing. "I love you."

"Marry me? Be my wife again. Be a Wilder in truth and in name and in everything."

"I'm already a Wilder, but I'll be yours, too," I whispered, and then I threw my arms around his neck. He caught me, kissing me softly. He slid both rings onto my finger, and I laughed, looking down at the two diamonds that were so varied in taste and in size, but I was varied, too. I wasn't the woman who had married him before. He wasn't the man I had married. But, now, we were exactly who we needed to be for each other.

And as he kissed me and walked me back to his bed, we slowly stripped each other of our clothing, naked together for the first time since the attack. He had needed time, and so had I. I hovered over him, slowly sliding over his length, he touched me, and I kissed him, and I rode him, both of us coming at the same time, whispering each other's names, the moonlight glinting off the diamonds on my fingers.

I was marrying my Wilder. My Evan.

I was marrying my best friend.

My ex-husband.

And the man I knew was my future. In this life and into the next.

Chapter Twenty-One

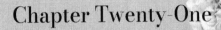

Evan

Wine poured, and people laughed, and I looked over at East and my fiancé, my wife, and my ex-wife, all the same person rolled into one, and shook my head.

"Are Kendall and East growling over who is the chef for the night again?" Everett asked as he stood by my side, the tone of his voice as if he were trying for humor. I looked at my brother, at the dark circles under his eyes, and didn't comment on them. Not today. We would speak soon, however. Because no matter how hypocritical it was for me to think, Everett couldn't be alone in his troubles for much longer.

I continued on as if my mind hadn't wandered. "I think they're cooking together. I honestly think East just wants to learn, and it makes Kendall smile."

"Well, he can cook, and that means I don't have to, so I'm happy with that," Everett added with a laugh.

Elijah walked around, pouring wine for everybody, and I chuckled, noticing the bounce in his step. Joy and Alexis were sitting on one of the small couches in Eli and Alexis' home, giggling with one another, and I understood why that pep was there.

That, and the reason we were having a Wilder dinner tonight.

"Okay, chefs, hold up your glasses. It's time for a toast," Elijah said, and I cleared my throat, knowing that we had already discussed this.

"To the Bliss clients who are back with us, finally."

"To the Bliss *sons*," Alexis added, and Kendall threw her head back and laughed.

"The Bliss sons who are not for *you*," Eli growled, and I just shook my head, my gaze on Kendall's.

I smiled as I sipped the wine, doing my best not to undress her with my eyes in front of my brothers.

"Daddy Bliss has decided no longer to be part of the

company," Elijah added. "And that means we have Bliss back, and Wilder Wines is better than ever."

I sipped the wine again, letting it settle on my tongue, and inhaled the deep scents.

"Better than ever."

"Between that, and LJ selling the Dodge resorts to another company? It's a good day," Everett put in.

I nodded, feeling a little bad about that part, because LJ had stepped up in the end. The rest of his family though? They were lucky I didn't want to break the wine glass in my hand.

"LJ's okay with it," Kendall put in as she walked over. "He's going to work with a few other companies and us, but he no longer has to be part of Dodge resorts. The new owners can clean it up however they want, and we don't have to be part of it." Kendall beamed, and I rolled my eyes, holding out my arm. She slid underneath it as if she had been there forever, and I just leaned into her, knowing that we had been through hell, but we had come out stronger for it. I would've liked not to go through so much hell along the way. But a man couldn't ask for too much. Not with the future we would have together.

"It's going to be nice, having LJ work with us, the Bliss brothers working with us, and us Wilders kicking ass," Eli said, as he held up his glass again.

"And, of course, we have a wedding to plan," Alexis added as she sipped her wine after the toast.

"Yes, and I can't wait to start planning with you," Joy added, clapping her hands. "I'm blessed that y'all are letting me help."

My fiancé blushed. "It'll be interesting doing a wedding like this on the grounds."

I leaned down and kissed the top of her head. "We can do whatever you want, Kendall."

"See, I'm only in the planning stages, but I'm pretty sure that's not what you say," Eli teased.

I rolled my eyes. "Thank you for that."

"I want you to plan with me," Kendall said. "Not every detail, but I want your opinion. Of course, we don't need a big wedding," she added quickly.

I shrugged. "I love you. I just want to call you my wife again."

The others in the room made an oooooh sound.

"We weren't there the first time, and Vegas with Elvis isn't exactly what you had in mind, did you?" Elliot asked, his mind going a thousand miles a minute from the look in his eyes. After all, he was a planner, even if he wasn't a wedding planner.

"It wasn't Elvis. It was Cher. Thank you very much," Kendall said snootily, and I laughed.

"Honestly, as long as you're my wife, I don't care

what we do. But any planning you need, I'll be there," I added at the look in her eyes. "I swear, I won't just show up the day of."

Kendall smiled. "Sounds like a plan. And the good thing is, we have the perfect place to have the wedding. And I know a good chef and a wedding planner, and oh look, I know exactly the wine that we'll have."

"Hear! Hear!" Elijah repeated, and I just rolled my eyes and pulled Kendall closer to me and pressed my mouth to hers.

"Love you," I whispered, still getting used to saying that phrase so often and aloud.

She grinned up at me. "I love you, too. Now, I need to get your brother out of the kitchen. Because he is not going to touch my macaroni and cheese." She shouted the last words in East's direction, and my brother just waved her off. She handed me her glass of wine and went back into the kitchen, scowling at something he was saying.

I leaned against the wall and watched my family laugh and come together. Our younger sister Eliza and her family would be here the next week, and then we would all be together. Some of us were further along in our healing and our futures than others, but we were making do.

But in the end, I always knew who was the one for me. I may have taken a wrong turn to get here, but I had found my way back.

With Kendall Wilder. My ex-wife. My love. And soon to be my wife.

BEFORE AND AFTER

Everett

"We have a full booking for the next month," Eli said as he went over his reports. I nodded and looked down at my notes.

"Which is good. Because we have a few updates to do. East will go over them with you."

"We still in the black?" Eli asked, brow raised.

I nodded. "We're doing good." I knocked on wood. "Though it could always be better."

"So I hear." Eli laughed.

"Anyway. Full bookings are good. Kendall's doing

302

well in the restaurant. The winery has its new label coming out. Alexis is working her ass off on the weddings, and Elliot is bouncing around from event to event. We've got it handled. We're right at the cusp of something. What? I don't know."

My brother just shook his head. "For somebody who's supposed to have their finger on the pulse of everything, shouldn't you know more?"

"I'm trying," I said with a laugh. "If we're done here, I'm starving, and I'm in the mood for mac and cheese."

"Does that mean Kendall left you some mac and cheese in your fridge that you're going to reheat?" Eli asked.

"I know exactly what I'm in the mood for, thank you very much."

Eli just laughed, and we put away our things, and I headed back to my cabin on the other side of the property. I liked living near my brothers, even though some of them were starting to move off into their own homes. But, for the first couple of years, when we were together and were focusing on the property and coming together as Wilders, it was nice. It felt like we knew what the hell we were doing—and getting to know one another again. Considering sometimes I felt like I didn't know myself when I looked in the mirror these days, that was good. It was hard for me to reconcile the fact that some memories from my past were never coming back. That getting my head knocked in the way that it had sometimes made the numbers on my screen swirl into a whirlpool, but I figured it out. All of my brothers had their own issues from their time in the service.

I wasn't the only one.

I went to work in my kitchen, hitting up the best five-cheese macaroni and cheese there was thanks to my former and soon to be current sister-in-law, and went through the rest of my to-do list for the next day.

I needed things to be in order. I had to go through my to-do list daily to make sure I didn't mess things up. I had notes all around the house to make sure that I was ready to go, and my phone was never not at my side. I never used to be like this. I used to remember everything, but now, having a checklist for my day was how I focused and how I'd made the best of it.

I was digging into the best macaroni and cheese of my life, even reheated, when my doorbell rang. I frowned and walked over, Tupperware still in my hand, and nearly dropped the whole thing when I opened it.

She stood there.

Bethany.

Her long brown hair framing her face, her bright eyes that sang to me.

Every time I saw those on the screen, I felt like I

knew her, felt like she was everything. It was such a weird goddam crush.

She stared at me as if searching for something and then narrowed her gaze.

"Bethany. Hi. I didn't know you were coming. Are you staying at the resort? Wait, do you need help figuring out where to go? I can get you to a cabin." I set down my macaroni and cheese.

She just shook her head, her eyes widening. "You really don't remember. You have no idea."

I blinked, wondering at the venom in her tone. "Remember? I remember you. Of course, I know who you are."

"Oh, you remember me from our walk, and what, from a movie or two? But, Everett, you don't remember the fact that we fucked?" she snarled, her gaze narrowing.

That dirty word coming out of that sweet mouth nearly rocked me to my core, and I looked at her, shaken.

Because there was no way I could have ever slept with Bethany Cole and not remembered.

Because I *knew* Bethany Cole.

I'd had that silly crush on that celebrity for far too long, and if I had ever touched Bethany Cole—other than holding her hand for a second to help lead her down the path when she had almost fallen off a brick walkway—I would have remembered.

"Are you sure you have the right brother?" I blurted, embarrassed. Because there were six of us, she could have slept with another Wilder brother. That made my stomach hurt, and yet I knew it was the wrong thing to say as soon as the hurt crossed her face.

"You're lucky I don't believe in hitting people because I could slap you for that. I know which Wilder I slept with, Everett. I just can't believe you don't remember. I thought you were one of the good ones. And then you walked away and never came back. And now look. You don't remember me, which is *fine*. It would probably be better if most people forgot me."

She whirled on her heels and stomped away, and I ran after her, gripping her elbow.

"Bethany. Are you serious?"

"Of course, I'm serious." Her eyes filled before she blinked it away, the steel temptress in place of the crying waif. "You don't know me. *Fine*. I get it. You don't want to remember that night? *Fine*. But don't lie to me. And don't treat me like shit. I am done being treated like shit by everybody who thinks that they own me because I am on their stupid video screens. Fuck you, Wilder."

"I don't remember," I whispered, grasping for any semblance of who I was before everything changed.

But I couldn't remember.

"Of course, you don't remember. We weren't drunk but, apparently, you forgot everything about that night like I was nothing."

I shook my head. "No. I don't remember."

"Fine. I'm so happy that you can forget. I'll do the same." Her eyes filled again, but she tried to turn away as if that could stop the memory of them searing into my brain.

Anger pounded my temples. But not at her. Never at her. "You didn't have your head nearly blown off when a bomb exploded near you. So, I'm sorry if I don't remember you. I don't even remember what my mom looks like without a fucking photo these days. I'm sorry. I wish I could goddamn well remember because that is something that I would want to remember. I'm sorry, Bethany. I don't remember. I'm sorry." My head pulsed, and I pressed my fingers down to my temples, taking a deep breath, trying to focus.

"Everett? Are you serious?" She moved forward, but I took a step back as a flash of memory assailed me, one after another.

A sweet smile.

A flash of lips.

A laugh that went right to my toes.

And then bile filled my throat, and I staggered to the

side. Bethany was saying something, screaming my name, or maybe she was whispering it. I didn't know. But I fell to my knees, and then her hands were on me, or maybe it was just a dream.

Just like a memory I had forgotten long ago.

And then there was nothing.

**

Next in the Wilder Brothers Series:
Things get interesting with Everett and
Bethany: The Path to You

If you'd like to read a bonus scene from Evan
& Kendall:
Check out this special Epilogue!

A Note from Carrie Ann Ryan

Thank you so much for reading **Always the One for Me.**

Evan and Kendall hurt my brain and my heart to write and yet at the same time, I couldn't let go. I'm honestly so happy with how their story came out!

If you'd like to read Eliza's story, you can find it in Inked Obsession!

The Wilder Brothers Series:

Book 1: One Way Back to Me
Book 2: Always the One for Me
Book 3: The Path to You
Book 4: Coming Home for Us
More to come!

Next in the Wilder Brothers Series:
Things get interesting with Everett and
Bethany: The Path to You

IF YOU'D LIKE TO READ A BONUS SCENE FROM EVAN
& KENDALL:
CHECK OUT THIS SPECIAL EPILOGUE!

If you want to make sure you know what's coming next from me, you can sign up for my newsletter at www. CarrieAnnRyan.com; follow me on twitter at @CarrieAnnRyan, or like my Facebook page. I also have a Facebook Fan Club where we have trivia, chats, and other goodies. You guys are the reason I get to do what I do and I thank you.

Make sure you're signed up for my MAILING LIST so you can know when the next releases are available as well as find giveaways and FREE READS.

Happy Reading!

Also from Carrie Ann Ryan

The Montgomery Ink Legacy Series:
Book 1: Bittersweet Promises
Book 2: At First Meet
Book 3: Longtime Crush

The Wilder Brothers Series:
Book 1: One Way Back to Me
Book 2: Always the One for Me
Book 3: The Path to You
Book 4: Coming Home for Us

The Aspen Pack Series:
Book 1: Etched in Honor
Book 2: Hunted in Darkness
Book 3: Mated in Chaos

Book 4: Harbored in Silence

The Montgomery Ink: Fort Collins Series:

Book 1: Inked Persuasion

Book 2: Inked Obsession

Book 3: Inked Devotion

Book 3.5: Nothing But Ink

Book 4: Inked Craving

Book 5: Inked Temptation

The Montgomery Ink: Boulder Series:

Book 1: Wrapped in Ink

Book 2: Sated in Ink

Book 3: Embraced in Ink

Book 3: Moments in Ink

Book 4: Seduced in Ink

Book 4.5: Captured in Ink

Book 4.7: Inked Fantasy

Book 4.8: A Very Montgomery Christmas

Montgomery Ink: Colorado Springs

Book 1: Fallen Ink

Book 2: Restless Ink

Book 2.5: Ashes to Ink

Book 3: Jagged Ink

Book 3.5: Ink by Numbers

Montgomery Ink Denver:

Book 0.5: Ink Inspired

Book 0.6: Ink Reunited

Book 1: Delicate Ink

Book 1.5: Forever Ink

Book 2: Tempting Boundaries

Book 3: Harder than Words

Book 3.5: Finally Found You

Book 4: Written in Ink

Book 4.5: Hidden Ink

Book 5: Ink Enduring

Book 6: Ink Exposed

Book 6.5: Adoring Ink

Book 6.6: Love, Honor, & Ink

Book 7: Inked Expressions

Book 7.3: Dropout

Book 7.5: Executive Ink

Book 8: Inked Memories

Book 8.5: Inked Nights

Book 8.7: Second Chance Ink

Book 8.5: Montgomery Midnight Kisses

Bonus: Inked Kingdom

The On My Own Series:

Book 0.5: My First Glance

Book 1: My One Night

Book 2: My Rebound
Book 3: My Next Play
Book 4: My Bad Decisions

The Promise Me Series:

Book 1: Forever Only Once
Book 2: From That Moment
Book 3: Far From Destined
Book 4: From Our First

The Less Than Series:

Book 1: Breathless With Her
Book 2: Reckless With You
Book 3: Shameless With Him

The Fractured Connections Series:

Book 1: Breaking Without You
Book 2: Shouldn't Have You
Book 3: Falling With You
Book 4: Taken With You

The Whiskey and Lies Series:

Book 1: Whiskey Secrets
Book 2: Whiskey Reveals
Book 3: Whiskey Undone

The Gallagher Brothers Series:

Book 1: Love Restored

Book 2: Passion Restored

Book 3: Hope Restored

The Ravenwood Coven Series:

Book 1: Dawn Unearthed

Book 2: Dusk Unveiled

Book 3: Evernight Unleashed

The Talon Pack:

Book 1: Tattered Loyalties

Book 2: An Alpha's Choice

Book 3: Mated in Mist

Book 4: Wolf Betrayed

Book 5: Fractured Silence

Book 6: Destiny Disgraced

Book 7: Eternal Mourning

Book 8: Strength Enduring

Book 9: Forever Broken

Book 10: Mated in Darkness

Book 11: Fated in Winter

Redwood Pack Series:

Book 1: An Alpha's Path

Book 2: A Taste for a Mate

Book 3: Trinity Bound
Book 3.5: A Night Away
Book 4: Enforcer's Redemption
Book 4.5: Blurred Expectations
Book 4.7: Forgiveness
Book 5: Shattered Emotions
Book 6: Hidden Destiny
Book 6.5: A Beta's Haven
Book 7: Fighting Fate
Book 7.5: Loving the Omega
Book 7.7: The Hunted Heart
Book 8: Wicked Wolf

The Elements of Five Series:

Book 1: From Breath and Ruin
Book 2: From Flame and Ash
Book 3: From Spirit and Binding
Book 4: From Shadow and Silence

Dante's Circle Series:

Book 1: Dust of My Wings
Book 2: Her Warriors' Three Wishes
Book 3: An Unlucky Moon
Book 3.5: His Choice
Book 4: Tangled Innocence
Book 5: Fierce Enchantment

Book 6: An Immortal's Song

Book 7: Prowled Darkness

Book 8: Dante's Circle Reborn

Holiday, Montana Series:

Book 1: Charmed Spirits

Book 2: Santa's Executive

Book 3: Finding Abigail

Book 4: Her Lucky Love

Book 5: Dreams of Ivory

The Branded Pack Series:
(Written with Alexandra Ivy)

Book 1: Stolen and Forgiven

Book 2: Abandoned and Unseen

Book 3: Buried and Shadowed

About the Author

Carrie Ann Ryan is the New York Times and USA Today bestselling author of contemporary, paranormal, and young adult romance. Her works include the Montgomery Ink, Redwood Pack, Fractured Connections, and Elements of Five series, which have sold over 3.0 million books worldwide. She started writing while in graduate school for her advanced degree in chemistry and hasn't stopped since. Carrie Ann has written over seventy-five novels and novellas with more in the works. When she's not losing herself in her emotional and action-packed worlds, she's reading as much as she can while wrangling her clowder of cats who have more followers than she does.

www.CarrieAnnRyan.com

Printed in Great Britain
by Amazon

84453810R10183